James Harrison Rigg

Churchmanship of John Wesley

And the Relations of Wesleyan Methodism to the Church of England

James Harrison Rigg

Churchmanship of John Wesley
And the Relations of Wesleyan Methodism to the Church of England

ISBN/EAN: 9783337372446

Printed in Europe, USA, Canada, Australia, Japan

Cover: Foto ©Raphael Reischuk / pixelio.de

More available books at **www.hansebooks.com**

THE

CHURCHMANSHIP OF

JOHN WESLEY,

AND THE

RELATIONS OF WESLEYAN METHODISM

TO THE CHURCH OF ENGLAND.

By JAMES H. RIGG, D.D.,

AUTHOR OF 'MODERN ANGLICAN THEOLOGY,' 'ESSAYS FOR THE TIMES,'
'THE LIVING WESLEY,' ETC.

NEW AND REVISED EDITION.

London:
PUBLISHED FOR THE AUTHOR AT THE
WESLEYAN-METHODIST BOOK-ROOM;
2, CASTLE-STREET, CITY-ROAD;
AND 66, PATERNOSTER-ROW.

PREFACE.

THE pages which follow have not been written primarily for Wesleyans, but for non-Wesleyans, for general students of history, for students, in particular, of ecclesiastical history, for all who desire to understand the opinions and character of John Wesley, and the precise position and relations of Wesleyan Methodism among the ecclesiastical organisations and communities of England, and, especially, for the information of earnest Churchmen, those, most of all, who look with concern and uneasiness on the 'schismatic' position and tendencies of modern Methodism.

I have avoided, accordingly, the use of specifically Methodist phraseology, and, though myself a Wesleyan, have, except here and there at a point of application or final inference, written rather as a general student, outside of Methodism, might write, than as one using the freemasonry of phrase and allusion peculiar to the 'people called Methodists.' This explanation I make more for the sake of Methodist readers than of any others.

The volume itself is a new composite out of materials the greater part of which have already been published. The substance of about one-half appeared in the *Contemporary Review*, in September, 1876, as an article on ' The Churchmanship of John Wesley.' By the courtesy of Mr, Strahan, I am allowed to use it for the purpose of this volume. Most of the remainder had appeared in a former publication on the ' Relations of John Wesley and Wesleyan Methodism to the Church of England,' which was called forth by special circumstances eleven years ago, and of which two editions have been sold, but which will be superseded by the present volume.

As now re-cast, these materials constitute a small volume which, as I venture to hope, will have a permanent interest, and will conduce, not to division and controversy, but to settlement and peace so far as regards the Church of England and Wesleyan Methodism with their mutual relations,

But far deeper and more abiding than any inter-denominational or controversial interest is that which belongs to the natural history and growth of the character and opinions of one of the most remarkable men and of the most influential personalities that the modern world has known. If I have been able to cast any new and steadfast light upon this subject, my little book will have some permanent value.

JAMES H. RIGG.

WESTMINSTER,
December 10th, 1878.

PREFACE TO THE PRESENT EDITION.

IN the present edition some corrections have · been made of minor importance, to which I need not particularly refer, and one of considerable importance. Mr. Telford, in his life of John Wesley, lately published * has proved that John Wesley was never in any sense a Moravian, and that the Fetter Lane Society, as he established it, was not a Moravian Society. I have consequently had to re-write some paragraphs in the third chapter of this volume. Elsewhere I have made a few changes or additions in order to bring the statistics and some of the references of the present edition up to date. The book, however, as a whole, remains unaltered. The argument is quite unaffected by such correc-

---

* *The Life of John Wesley.* By the Rev. J. Telford, B.A. (Hodder and Stoughton.)

tions as I have made in this edition. The reader will please to remember, especially in reading the introductory chapter, that the volume was first published more than ten years back, and that much of it was written, and indeed published, several years earlier. I have not thought it necessary or desirable to alter the time-references generally so as to accommodate them to the present year. The case is the same as it was ten or twenty years ago. The situation has in no respect materially altered.

It is gratifying to know that the volume has not been written in vain. It has been recognised, and its argument accepted practically, if not with explicit acknowledgment, by some of the most distinguished recent authorities on the history of the Church of England since the rise of Methodism. There are still to be found a few writers who cavil, more or less, at its conclusions. But they do not meet its arguments, nor are they authorities on whom the standard historians of England or the English Church, now or hereafter, will rely for either opinion or information.

JAMES H. RIGG.

Westminster,
Christmas Eve, 1886.

CONTENTS.

THE CHURCHMANSHIP OF

JOHN WESLEY,

AND THE

RELATIONS OF WESLEYAN METHODISM TO THE CHURCH OF ENGLAND.

CHAPTER I.

INTRODUCTORY.

WESLEY'S opinions as to questions of ecclesiastical principle are interesting to the philosophical historian or biographer in their own right, as I trust the following pages will show. There are few more curious or more instructive studies in the development of character and opinion than the study of Wesley's mind as his views in regard to church principles and polity varied from period to period of his course, in accordance with the changes of his theological sympathies and opinions, until at length he settled down permanently into the position which he held for almost half a century at the head of

B

the Methodist Conference and of 'the people called Methodists'; during nearly the whole of which prolonged period his ecclesiastical opinions varied as little as his theology.

But, for another reason also, it is a matter of interest and importance that the history of Wesley's ecclesiastical opinions and the matured form which they permanently assumed during the later and much the longer period of his life, should be conclusively investigated and determined. It is in regard to this point, beyond any other, that Churchmen are accustomed to press Wesleyans, pleading against the modern position and claims of Methodism the opinions and authority of John Wesley. This aspect of the subject, accordingly, as possessing some polemical importance, is the one which excites the keenest present interest, although the other aspect—that which belongs to the province of the philosophical biographer or historian—is the one which possesses much the greater permanent and intrinsic importance.

In the following pages the subject will be regarded from both points of view. Some introductory remarks relating to the question in its inter-denominational and more controversial aspect will occupy the remainder of this chapter, and will clear the way for the strictly historical chapters that are to follow.

One of the very noteworthy facts of the present age is the perseverance with which attempts are made, on the part of the Church by law established in England, to bring back the Wesleyan Methodists into communion with that Church. If, indeed, there was any possibility of such an attempt succeeding, nothing would be more natural than that it should be made. But the peculiarity of this case is, that there is no such possibility ; that the reasons which prove the impossibility are clear, and absolutely decisive ; that these reasons have been again and again set forth by the literary and connexional organs of Wesleyan Methodism, and by individual writers of eminence and authority ; and that the overtures and attempts on the part of the Established Church appear to have been made without any encouragement whatever from the expressed sentiments of any known Wesleyan, whether in speaking or in writing. It is yet more remarkable that in the letters, the pamphlets, and the discussions in Convocation, relating to this subject, the question is never raised as to how the Wesleyans have received former overtures, or whether their authorities have

ever pronounced upon this subject of reunion
with the Church of England. It seems as
if this were a point not worth inquiring about.
The *Wesleyan Magazine*, the *London Quarterly
Review*, the *Watchman* newspaper, have repeatedly, during the last twenty years, discussed
this subject in detail with complete frankness,
with an explicitness and fulness which could
leave no doubt on any point; but all this is
ignored. The venerable Thomas Jackson, a
Methodist of the elder school, was not less
explicit nearly forty years ago in his pamphlet,
Why are You a Wesleyan Methodist? than the
Rev. W. Arthur was twenty years ago in the
pages of the quarterly journal to which I have
just referred, in denying, with ample reasons
assigned, that there can be for the Church of
England any place for repentance in regard to
its rejection of Methodism from its borders,
or for Methodism itself any possibility of organic union with the Church of England.
And yet it would seem as if almost every
Churchman regarded it as a thing of course,
that, if the Church to which he belongs can
but show the way to attach Methodism to
itself as a privileged dependency, Methodism
will only be too happy to be absorbed. The
leading ministers, it seems to be imagined,
would feel it to be a wonderful elevation and

consolation to themselves, if episcopal hands could be laid on their heads ; the ministerial commonalty would be content to abdicate their pastoral character, and subside into preaching laymen—constituting a kind of subdiaconate —provided only that the hope of attaining to ordination· might rise before them in the distance; the people, like sequacious sheep, would *en masse* humbly follow their preachers into the Anglican fold ; trustees would make no question or scruple about the deeds by which the chapels are secured to the Wesleyan Connexion, and for the ministrations of Wesleyan itinerant preachers; the Methodism of England would be more than content, for the sake of union with the ancient and established Church of this English realm, the territorial and endowed and decorated Church of the Queen and Parliament, to sever itself from union and communion with the Methodism of all countries besides, and thus to mar the integrity of the greatest sisterhood of evangelical churches which the world has known ; nay, would be ready to isolate itself, as the Church of England is isolated, from the entire family of Reformed Christian churches of every nation ; and Parliament would be forward to dispose of all legal difficulties, and to ease the way to the recommunion and absorption desired.

All this, I repeat, is very surprising, and, on the whole, by no means flattering to the self-respect of the Wesleyan Connexion. It is as though a fashionable gentleman of noble family and extensive property had again and again sought the hand of a lady of middle rank and of country breeding, but of good looks and good property, and notwithstanding repeated and most decisive refusals, still persisted in his overtures with bland assumption, as if no denial had been given to his suit, or rather continued to write letters of inquiry as to the time, the place, and all other arrangements for the marriage, as though his rejection by the lady were a thing inconceivable, as if her refusal of such a personage as himself had been a mere ignorant mistake which could never be allowed to stand.*

I recommend Churchmen in general, who feel any interest in this subject, for their own sakes to procure Mr. Jackson's and Mr. Arthur's excellent publications, of which the titles will be found in the Appendix at the

---

* The passage in the text was first published *before* Dr. Pusey addressed his letter to the Rev. J. Bedford, the President of the Wesleyan Conference, during its Session in 1868, and before the cartoon and verses relating to that letter and to the answer of the Conference had appeared in a facetious contemporary journal.

end of this volume. I may also be allowed to quote here, for the sake of Churchmen, my own deliberate testimony, printed in 1866, in a volume entitled *Essays for the Times.* ' I have no hesitation,' I then said, 'in saying that there is not the remotest possibility of the Wesleyan Methodist Church ever being absorbed in the Church of England. And I doubt whether out of the many hundreds of Wesleyan ministers, and of the hundreds of thousands of Wesleyan communicants, there are altogether a score of persons who would not smile with supreme amusement if such a proposal were presented to them.' *

Let me not be misunderstood. Neither myself, nor any of the authorities to whom I have referred, must be supposed to be indifferent to the question of Christian union. If the proposal were in very deed one for drawing close the bonds of union between Christians of all denominations, or for establishing, as the late Dean Alford and as Dean Stanley have sought to establish, intercommunion on equal and fraternal terms between the Church of England and Nonconformist churches, the Wesleyan Church included, all that might be done in favour of it would be gladly done by such men as the late

* *Essays, &c.,* p. 1, 2. See also a very powerful paper in the *Wesleyan Magazine* for June, 1856.

Mr. Jackson and as Mr. Arthur, and,I hope I
may add, by myself. But what has been so often
talked of in Church Congress or Convocation,
what has been suggested in so many letters
and pamphlets, is not any union of churches,
as such, or any fraternal recognition or
intercommunion between the Episcopalian
clergy and the pastors of Wesleyan or other
Nonconformist churches, or anything, in a
word, which would imply an acknowledgment
of non-episcopal denominations as true Christian churches, or Nonconformist ministers as
true ministers of Christ, but merely the reab-
sorption of the denominations into the Established Church, by the submission of their clergy
to pass under the yoke of ecclesiastical depend-
ence, and by the subordination of all the rules
and privileges of the denominations to the
clerical assumptions and prerogatives of the
high Episcopalian theory. The bearing of the
advocates of what is called reunion towards the
Greek Church is most deferential, not to say
obsequious ; in this case what is contemplated
is a real reunion of churches on terms of
honour and equality for both parties, and without disbanding or subordination on the part
of either. The proposals on the part of the
Church of England in regard to Wesleyan
Methodism, which have from time to time

been brought forward, are altogether of a different character. If Wesleyans accordingly regard them with an interest which, although not unkindly, is rather critical than cordial or grateful, they must not on that account be condemned as indifferent to the question of Christian union. None long for such union more ardently than they—perhaps none are so favourably situated for realising it; if only the obstacles which arise from error and misconception as to the principles and feelings of the Methodist ministers and people can be removed.

That such obstacles should be removed is, however, of the highest importance. At present Wesleyans are apt to feel themselves affronted by the condescending overtures of Churchmen. When the latter intimate their hopes of a closer union with Wesleyans, Wesleyans themselves understand that the dissolution of their church-existence is held in view ; and Wesleyan ministers who use any expression of friendly regard towards the Church of England, or even towards particular efforts and undertakings connected with that Church, are liable to be annoyed and humiliated by finding their friendliness construed into a willingness to see the way made open for their return into the ' bosom of the Establishment.' I have undertaken the discussion, at this time,

of the question of reunion, or absorption, as
it respects Wesleyans in particular, in the hope
that I may set it at rest by a fundamental
investigation, and to show that the aims and
hopes of the well-meaning men who are
perpetually raising it rest upon a tissue of
fallacies and illusions.

Why do Churchmen perpetually single out
Wesleyan Methodism from among the denominations as the one to be absorbed? Its
mass and unity, no doubt, attract their admiration. Congregational churches could only
be annexed one by one; Congregational pastors would hardly be likely to go over in a
mass. But Methodism acts collectively: and,
if it could be imagined that the body as a
whole, under the leading of the Conference,
could be brought back into the Church of
England, of course the gain would be immense,
especially in these times of schism and dis-
traction within that Church. But might it not
naturally occur to Churchmen that the vaster
the system, the more highly organised in its
unity, the more complete in its manifold integrity, the more massive in the bulk of property which it holds, the more multitudinous
in its aggregate of churches and congregations, so much the more improbable it must
be that it could ever be brought to consent

to be reduced by absorption to the condition of a mere dependency within a church, with its pastors, except such as might have received the privilege of re-ordination, reduced to the rank of laydeacons, and its various, and independent life suppressed within the limits of a mere ecclesiastical order, sanctioned in its irregularity, but inferior and subordinate, subject to Anglo-episcopal control, and adjusted in some way to the framework of the Established Church, with its antique system of prescription and stereotype?

In 1856, indeed, the self-constituted committee for promoting the absorption of Methodism into the Church of England took encouragement from the fact that Methodists have never professed themselves Dissenters; and it is likely that the same consideration has still some weight with Churchmen. The reasons, however, for the intermediate position occupied by Methodism are sufficiently plain. Methodism did not originate in any active Dissent, and does not now require of its members, or even its ministers, any profession of Dissent, from the Church of England. It grew into a separate body, almost unconsciously, and very reluctantly, by a process of separate development, the steps of which I shall presently enumerate. Neither does Methodism understand that it is any part of its duty to profess any polemic principle, or to assume any offensive or critical position in regard to the Establishment, or any other Christian communion. In the eye of the law the Methodists may be regarded as Dissenters; but they raise, as Methodists, no question of political relation, or of ritual or doctrine, as regards the Church by law established. A day may come when the connection between Church and State in this country will be at an end. The designation ' Dissenters ' will then be out of date and out of place—(there are no Dissenters in America)—but the positive principles of Wesleyan Methodism will still remain.

It is a fact, indeed, that, some years ago, a distinguished Methodist minister gave evidence before a Committee of the House of Lords in favour of Church-rates, and incidentally also in support of the Church of England, as an eminently valuable religious and political institution. But it must be remembered that that evidence was given on the sole and personal responsibility of the witness. I have elsewhere set down my own assurance, that ' undoubtedly the great majority of Wesleyans were passively opposed to Church-rates; they heartily disliked them, although few of them may have joined in any agitation against them.'* And in an able and temperate paper published in the *Wesleyan Magazine* for April, 1868, and understood to be from the pen of the distinguished minister to whom I have referred, which deals with the very subject of ' The Union of the Methodists with the Church of England,' I find the following passage :—

'We hope it now appears that in every point of view these proposals for union are impracticable, ill-considered, and inexpedient. If those who make them would expend their time and talent in maintaining the Protestant character of the Established Church, they would do far more (though indirectly) towards accomplishing their object than by any such overtures as we have lately heard of. They would conciliate the feelings of many now grieved, beyond expression, at the unfaithfulness of those who claim to be the only authorised guides and instructors of the English people. Another method of usefulness in the same direction is open to them. They may, in their several neighbourhoods, treat their Methodist neighbours with gentleness and consideration, and respect their legal rights and liberties. Many of the clergy appear to think a Methodist preacher a being almost beneath notice, and debarred from the courtesies of society. Union in a smaller sphere they do not contemplate, though they talk about it on a large scale. Wisdom, however, would reverse this course of proceeding, and proceed from less to more. Nothing is lost by civility ; something may be gained by it.'

* *Essays, &c.*, p. 7.

There can be no greater mistake, indeed, than to suppose that there is, or ever has been, at least in the present generation, any party within Methodism, whether of ministers or among the people, who have felt the slightest concern as to union with the Church of England. Such a union has been regarded as simply out of the question. There has never been within my knowledge the faintest movement in its favour. It was a complaint of Mr. Crowther,* in 1795, that the 'children of Methodists, alas! too seldom grow up Methodists.' It is not an uncommon complaint of Methodists to-day that their children, when they grow up, migrate into the Church of England. On the whole, however, the attachment of Methodists to their own denomination is firmer now than at any former period. And, so far as I am able to judge, the number of young persons brought up among the Congregationalist Nonconformists who pass across into the ranks of the more fashionable and ecclesiastically open and undisciplined State Church, is not smaller than of the children of Methodists. So, also, the number of ministers now in the Church of England who received their early training (in some instances

* The elder Jonathan Crowther, one of Wesley's preachers.

as ministerial candidates) in the ranks of Congregational Dissent is probably larger in proportion than of those who passed their early
years in Methodism. It is scarcely to be
questioned that more ministers of mature age
and respectable position pass over to the
Church of England from the Independents
and Baptists than from the Methodists. The
Rev. George Venables, in his paper on Nonconformists and the Church, read before the
Church Congress of 1867, speaks, in a series
of notes, of a ' Dissenter of high position, who
wishes to conform,' to whom he is indebted
for ' courteous letters ' on the subject; of a
' Nonconformist of position and ability,' to
whom he had written, and ' who would join
the Communion of the Church at once, but
by no means alone, if one or two suggested
explanations were given;' of a ' Nonconformist
minister,' with whom he has been in correspondence, ' who desires to cease his Nonconformity, if only some fair opportunity were
given him by the Church '; of ' a very eminent
Dissenting minister' (now deceased), who 'told
him that if he had his time over again, he
would be ordained in the Church of England.'
This minister, it may be probably inferred
from an allusion on a foregoing page of Mr.
Venables' paper, was the late Rev. John

Clayton; and Mr. Venables professes to be 'rather intimately acquainted with Dissent (though never connected with it), and to have been at one time well known to a few of its eminent ministers.' Now, it is to be noted that we never hear of such confidential communications as these having been made by Wesleyan ministers to clergymen of the Church of England.

I imagine, however, that that which most powerfully influences clergymen in their advances upon the Methodist Church is the consideration that John Wesley, till his death, considered himself as belonging to the Church of which he was ordained a minister, and wished and urged his people, as far as possible, to attend her services and take part in her communion. It is hence inferred that Methodists ought to be members of the Church of England, if they duly revere their founder's memory and precepts, and that there can be no insuperable difficulty in effecting their return. The inference, indeed, is eminently fallacious. The Methodists were forced by circumstances to widen the separation, already in reality radical, although in extent only partial and in appearance not very considerable, which, sorely against his will, Wesley had been obliged to make between his societies and the Church of

England. Half a century ago, this separation
may be said to have become universal and
complete, and fifty years of growth since
that time must needs have built up a system
which cannot now be folded back within the
precincts of the Church of England. 'New
bottles' have been provided for the 'new
wine'; to attempt to pour it back into the
'old bottles' would be insanity. Still the
fallacy I have spoken of does prevail. Mr.
Wesley's principles and conduct, and the
relations of Methodism to the Church of
England during the later years of Wesley,
are, indeed, altogether misunderstood. One
object of this publication is to dispose effectu-
ally of the assumptions and illusions of clergymen on this subject. The evidence offered in
the historical investigation which forms the
substance of the following chapters will, I
hope, set at rest the questions that have
hitherto been debated respecting the churchmanship of John Wesley.

CHAPTER II

WESLEY'S CHURCHMANSHIP IN HIS EARLIER LIFE.

PERIOD OF RITUALISTIC HIGH CHURCHMANSHIP, 1725-1738—WESLEY'S CONVERSION.

THE Methodism of to-day will never be understood until the history of its founder is rightly understood ; and neither the history of Wesley himself, nor the character of his life-work, can ever be understood until it is recognised that his life was divided into two distinct, and in many respects sharply-contrasted, periods—the period preceding and the period following the spring of 1738. The opinions of his earlier years have often been attributed to him as his permanent convictions and principles, although he had abandoned them fifty years before his death, while the real principles which guided all his course as the founder of Methodism have apparently never been apprehended at all by many who have undertaken to pronounce on the subject both of Wesley himself and of the community which he founded. It is my purpose in the present volume to exhibit as clearly as I can what Wesley was, as a Churchman, before the

turning-point in his history, and what he afterwards became, and to indicate also, at least in
part, how the Methodism which he founded has
been moulded, and its ecclesiastical position
determined, by the principles which he adopted
after the spring of 1738.

Wesley's parents were of the Church of
England and were High Church : but their
ancestors, so far back as we can trace, had been
Puritans : in the last generation indeed had
been Nonconformists. The Wesleys or West-
leys, were a line of Puritan clergymen in
Wessex (Dorsetshire seems to have been their
centre), men of decided views, but of liberal
culture, Oxford being their hereditary University. Both the father and the grandfather of
the Epworth rector had suffered for their
opinions, the father in particular (John West-
ley) having been much harassed, and more
than once imprisoned. Susanna Wesley, the
rector's wife, came of a courtly and town-bred
race of Puritan clergy ; and her father, Dr
Annesley, though a leader among the Nonconformists, seems to have suffered little personal
hardship. Both the rector and his wife, however, had in their early youth abandoned Puri-
tanism, or rather Dissent. Mr. Wesley became a strict, but yet, like many of the clergy
of that period, a time-serving Churchman, the

colour of whose ecclesiastical opinions always matched the shade which for the time found favour at Court. He was naturally much disliked by the Dissenters as a deserter from their camp, and, in his earlier life, he returned their dislike in full; but, in his old age, he and they appear to have come to something like friendly terms. Wesley's mother, on the other hand, was throughout life a Jacobite High-Churchwoman, whose ecclesiastical creed was a matter of passionate sentiment and affection, and was cherished as warmly under Low Church William as during Queen Anne's High Church *régime*. Both parents were strict disciplinarians: the rector in his parish, where loose livers were taught to fear the Church courts; and the mother in her family, where, however, she seems to have united, in a remarkable manner, at least for that age, the minimum of punishment with the maximum of authority and order.

Coming from such a stock, and having been bred up in habits of frugal stint as well as strict discipline at home, and of patient and hardy endurance at the Charterhouse School, Wesley went to Oxford in 1720, and, having taken orders in 1725, appears to have begun his clerical course as a moderate theologian. His first theological counsellors were, naturally, his parents. The rector was never a High Church theologian, whatever ecclesiastical line he might, at certain periods, take in Convocation. Nor did his mother's Jacobitism affect her theology. She believed in the divine right of kings, and probably also of bishops, but she did not accept the theology of Laud or of Sheldon. From the first the younger Wesley rejected Calvinism, and insisted also that Christians in a state of salvation must be happily conscious of the fact. He distinctly rejected also the doctrine, extensively held at that day, of the 'conversion of the elements,' the modern 'Anglo-Catholic' doctrine of the 'real presence.' He said, twenty years later, of his own preaching and belief at this time (1725—1729)—

'I preached much, but saw no fruit of my labour. Indeed it could not be that I should, for I neither laid the foundation of repentance nor of preaching the Gospel, taking it for granted that all to whom I preached were believers, and that many of them needed no repentance.'*

In 1729, however, having been deeply impressed by reading Law's *Serious Call*, Wesley joined the original Methodist company at Oxford, which, during his absence in Lincolnshire, where he had been serving his father's rectory

* *Works*, viii., p. 450.

of Wroote (held with Epworth), had been founded by his brother Charles and by some other University men, chiefly undergraduates. From this time Wesley's doctrines became more intense and more severe. He laid now, as he himself wrote in 1746,* 'a deeper foundation of repentance,' but he knew nothing as yet of the ' evangelical' doctrines of ' reconciliation' and 'justification.' He insisted—following in this his teacher Law—on a high standard of religious consecration and personal holiness, both active and passive. He presently united with these views not a little of the High Church doctrine and discipline.

Mr. Tyerman's interesting volume, entitled *The Oxford Methodists,* enables us to trace with great distinctness the stages by which Wesley's religious earnestness developed into punctilious and ascetic ritualism. William Morgan, one of the very first Methodists—a true Keltic devotee—was an intense ascetic. Wesley learnt his asceticism from Morgan, who, however, died in 1732. In the same year John Clayton joined the Methodist company. From his example, and the influence of the friends to whom he introduced Wesley, especially Dr. Deacon, a learned High Church Jacobite, of repute in his day, Wesley seems to have im-

* *Works,* viii., p. 451.

bibed what would now be called ritualism in
an extreme form. Mr. Tyerman publishes a
curious correspondence with Clayton, which
brings this out very clearly. The close intimacy
of Wesley and Clayton covers the interval
1732-- 1735, and their warm friendship lasted
till 1738, when Wesley adopted the doctrines
of ' salvation by faith.' Through Clayton and
Deacon, Wesley was led for a time to follow
the guidance in matters ecclesiastical of the
pretended *Apostolical Constitutions*. Clayton,
as well as Deacon, was an intense Jacobite.
We have already noted that Wesley's mother
was a Jacobite Churchwoman.

But there was another influence besides
that of ritualism which told powerfully upon
Wesley between 1732 and 1735, the influence
of the Mystics, to whose fellowship he had been
introduced through William Law. Law was
himself a Jacobite of the most extreme type—a
Nonjuror ; this fact may have helped his influence over the minds of such men as Clayton,
and, in some measure also, over that of Wesley.
The main cause, however, of his influence over
Wesley was undoubtedly his *Serious Call* and
his *Christian Perfection*, both of which are
books of extraordinary power—the former
having been the means of profoundly impress-
ing the mind not only of Wesley but of Dr.

Johnson. Once established, Law's influence thoroughly penetrated Wesley, so that for some years Law was to him as an oracle.

Wesley was already an ascetic, when in 1732, several years after reading the *Serious Call*, he first paid a personal visit to Law ; he was also fast drifting into extreme ritualism. Nevertheless, the influence of Law must, on the whole, have been contrary to that of Clayton, and was no doubt really more profound, although for some years ritualism appeared to have the ascendency. Mysticism is often united with asceticism, with which indeed it would seem to have a natural affinity, but it is unquestionably opposed to a servile ritualism. Whether Mystic or Ritualist, Wesley was ascetic, and ascetic he remained after he had forsworn the fellowship alike of his early oracle Law and of his Jacobite High Church guide Clayton. Law recommended Wesley to read Tauler's works, the *Theologia Germanica,* and other similar writings. In reading them he must have found himself in a very different atmosphere from that of the *Apostolical Constitutions.*

Wesley has himself furnished us with an instructive comparative summary of the effects produced on his own mind and character, on the one hand by the acceptance of patristic traditionalism, as held by Clayton and his fellows, and on the other hand, by yielding to the spell of Law's mystical teachings.

On January 25th, 1738, on his voyage from Georgia, he wrote in a private paper:

'I bent the bow,' he says, 'too far the other way: 1. By making Antiquity a co-ordinate rather than subordinate rule with Scripture. 2. By admitting several doubtful writings, as undoubted evidences of Antiquity. 3. By extending Antiquity too far, even to the middle or end of the fourth century. 4. By believing more practices to have been universal in the ancient Church than ever were so. 5. By not considering that the Decrees of one Provincial Synod, could bind only that Province; and the Decrees of a general Synod, only those Provinces whose representatives met therein. 6. By not considering that the most of those Decrees were adapted to particular times and occasions; and consequently, when those occasions ceased, must cease to bind even those Provinces.' 'These considerations,' Wesley adds, 'insensibly stole upon me as I grew acquainted with the mystic writers, whose noble descriptions of union with God and internal religion made everything else appear mean, flat, and insipid. But in truth they make good works appear so too; yea, and faith itself, and what not?'*

Under this singular combination of influences, partly ritualistic, partly mystical, and whether ritualistic or mystical, always ascetic, Wesley remained during his 'Methodist' life

* *Whitehead's Wesley,* ii., 56.

—his University and pre-evangelical Methodist life—at Oxford. It was during this precise period that he was in love and in correspondence with the fascinating and celebrated Mrs. Pendarves, afterwards Mrs. Delany, a most interesting episode in his history, shedding a curious and unexpected light on his primary disposition and character. I have sketched this episode in one of the chapters of another volume,* but must not dwell upon it here.

Wesley himself, a few years afterwards, describes his manner of life at this time as a 'refined way of trusting to his own works and his own righteousness,' and says that he 'dragged on heavily, finding no help or comfort therein.'† He also speaks very distinctly as to the nature of the struggle within him between mysticism and a scrupulous practical conscience.

'Though,' he says, 'I could never fully come into this [the quietude of mysticism] nor contentedly omit what God enjoined; yet, I know not how, I fluctuated between obedience and disobedience. I had no heart, no vigour, no zeal in obeying; continually doubting whether I was right or wrong, and never out of perplexities and entanglements. Nor can I at this hour give a distinct account how I came back a little toward the right way; only my present sense is this—all the other enemies of Christianity are triflers; the Mystics

* *The Living Wesley.*   † *Works*, i., p. 94.

are the most dangerous of its enemies. They stab it in the vitals ; and its most serious professors are most likely to fall by them. May I praise Him who hath snatched me out of this fire likewise, by warning all others, that it is set on fire of hell !' *

So Wesley wrote in the beginning of 1738, on his return from America, but before he had fully embraced the doctrines of ' salvation by faith ' as afterwards expounded by himself and his followers. It appears to have been during his residence in America that Wesley finally broke with mysticism. There can be no doubt, however, that the element of truth in the mystical teaching remained by him ; and that his philosophy and theology were permanently elevated and enriched through the familiarity which he had gained with some, at least, of the writers to whom Law had introduced him, as well as through the direct influence of Law himself.

One conclusion results from all the evidence on this subject, viz., that though Wesley was a High Church Ritualist at Oxford, he was never a fully-persuaded or single-minded Ritualist. With him it was during these years a struggle between ritualism and mysticism ; and that struggle was not finally ended until he found in the personal Christian faith of an

* *Whitehead's Wesley*, vol. ii., p. 57.

evangelical Arminian Churchman that which, to him at least, afforded the real and abiding rest which mystic quietism could but simulate; until he came under the sway of that ' law of the Spirit of life in Christ Jesus ' which kept alive the continual spirit of devotion, and sustained from within that outward service of Christian worship and beneficence which he had previously struggled to maintain in full energy by an almost unintermitted round of self-imposed observances and duties.

No part of Wesley's life is more interesting to the student of character and its development, or to one who desires to trace the actual growth of his opinions, than that which immediately followed this period at Oxford—the interval, namely, which he passed in America and on the voyages to and fro. Here, again, I must abstain from more than a passing reference to his relations with an attractive woman, to his celebrated ' affair of the heart ' with Miss Hopkey in Georgia. Of this subject also I have written in my volume on *The Living Wesley.* It is needful, however, to mention the fact that Wesley's failure to prosecute his love-suit with Miss Hopkey involved him in an ecclesiastical law-suit, and was to him the beginning of troubles in the colony. Enemies rose up against him, and he was publicly indicted as

having been guilty of sundry illegal and inju-
rious acts of ecclesiastical despotism. The
law-suit entirely broke down, but the indict-
ment, taken in connection with his own ad-
missions and comments, instructs us as to the
character of his churchmanship at this period.
The resemblance of his practices to those of
modern High Anglicans is, in not a few points,
exceedingly striking. He had early and also
forenoon service every day; he divided the
morning service, taking the Litany as a
separate service; he inculcated fasting, and
weekly communion, requiring those who intended to take the sacrament to prepare themselves for its reception by taking private
counsel with himself;* he refused the Lord's

* It is perhaps not quite certain that Wesley at
this or at any time made private confession to the
priest as a preparation for the Lord's Supper a part of
his fixed discipline. Some evidence on the subject may
be found in Tyerman's *Oxford Methodists*, especially in
his account of the Jacobite churchman, Mr. Clayton,
and in Tyerman's *Life of Wesley*, from which (vol. i. p.
94) is taken the following extract of a letter from his
sister Emilia to himself. The extract shows at least
that at one period he had put pressure upon his sister
to use confession, and the evidence in the *Oxford
Methodists* shows that the friends at the University
made such a familiar use of the word *confessor* in
speaking of persons of their acquaintance as implied
that the practice of private confession in their circles
was customary. Emilia Wesley writes, ' To lay open
the state of my soul to you, or any of our clergy, is
what I have no inclination to do at present; and

Supper to all who had not been baptized by a minister episcopally ordained; he insisted on baptism by immersion; he rebaptized the children of Dissenters; and he refused to bury all who had not received episcopalian baptism. One main point, however, was wanting to make the parallel with our moderns complete; there is no evidence that he believed in the ' conversion of the elements ' by consecration, or in their doctrine of the real presence.*

Indeed, I shall very soon show that at no time did he believe this tenet of Anglican Neo-Popery. He was of course at this time a believer in the ' three orders ' of the priesthood and in apostolical succession. I may add to my picture some touches from the pen of Thomas Jackson, the author of *The Life of Charles Wesley*, and the very accurate editor of Wesley's works, who in his introduction to

I believe I never shall. I shall not put my conscience under the direction of mortal man frail as myself. To my own Master I stand or fall. Nay, I scruple not to say that all such desire in you or any other ecclesiastic seems to me like Church tyranny, and assuming to yourselves a dominion over your fellow creatures which was never designed you by God.'

* Under date February 28th, 1732, Wesley thus writes to his mother : ' One consideration is enough to make me assent to his (*i.e.* his father's) and your judgment concerning the holy sacrament; which is, that we cannot allow Christ's human nature to be present in it, without allowing either CON- or TRANS-substantiation.' *Works*, xii., p. 13.

Lockwood's *Life of Peter Böhler*, tells us that in Georgia Wesley ' turned his face to the East when he recited the creed, most probably mixed the sacramental wine with water, prayed standing on Whit-Sunday, and certainly deemed himself a Sacrificing Priest.'

It is well known that Wesley refused the Lord's Supper to one of the most exemplary Christians in the colony, John Martin Bolzius, the pastor of the Salzburgers, because he had not been, as Wesley insisted, canonically baptized. His entry in his journal in reference to this matter, written many years later, is very noteworthy. It ends with the words, ' Can anyone carry High Church zeal higher than this ? And how well have I since been beaten with mine own staff!'* In regard to this matter there is the following entry in Wesley's unpublished journal under date, Sunday, July 17th, 1737 :—' I had occasion to make a very unusual trial of the temper of Mr. Bolzius, in which he behaved with such lowliness and meekness as became a disciple of Jesus Christ.'

With all his High Church intolerance, however, Wesley in Georgia was inwardly melting. His intercourse with Moravians, on the voyage out and in the colony, deeply impressed him. He did not admire or approve

* *Journal*, September 29th, 1749.

all their peculiarities, but they seemed to have found the rest which he had so long sought in vain. He remarked with special admiration that they were delivered even from the fear of death—a fear which continually overcast Wesley at this time of his life, although afterwards he was so completely delivered from it. He learnt something also, in Georgia, from the Lutheran Salzburgers. Moreover, he attended a Presbyterian service at Darien, and there, to his great astonishment, heard the minister offer a devout and appropriate extempore prayer. He was present at a meeting of the clergy of the neighbouring province of South Carolina, at which, he says in his diary, 'there was such a conversation, for several hours, on "Christ our Righteousness and Example," with such seriousness and closeness as I never heard in England, in all the visitations I have been present at.'

'I entirely agree with you,' thus he wrote to a friend, 'that religion is love, and peace, and joy in the Holy Ghost; that as it is the happiest, so it is the cheerfulest thing in the world; that it is utterly inconsistent with moroseness, sourness, severity, and indeed whatever is not according to the softness, sweetness, and gentleness of Christ Jesus. I believe it is equally contrary to all preciseness, stiffness, affectation, and unnecessary singularity. I allow, too, that prudence, as well as zeal, is of the most importance in the Christian life. But I do

not yet see any possible case wherein trifling conversation can be an instance of it. . . . I am not for an
austere manner of conversing. No; let all the cheer-
fulness of faith be there, all the joyfulness of hope, all
the amiable sweetness, the winning easiness of love. If
we must have art, " Hæc mihi erunt artes." '*

It was, in fact, the gradual rise within him,
even in Georgia, of evangelical views and sympathies—I need hardly say that I use the
word *evangelical* in no narrow sense—which
slowly dispelled the mystical confusion that
had so long beclouded him. During the latter
part, at any rate, of his American experience,
it is evident that underneath the outward rule
both of rubrical observance and of ascetic
discipline, which was maintained with such un-
relenting severity—and, perhaps, with all the
more severity because of his inward rebel-
lion against the yoke—there was welling up
within him a fountain of true Christian self-
knowledge and a passionate longing after a new
life.

He left Georgia ' a sadder and a wiser
man ' than he had entered it. His voyage
home was a season of sorrowful review and
self-searching. He had good right, indeed,
to feel humbled. As yet he appeared to have
failed in everything he had had at heart since

* Tyerman's *Life of Wesley*, vol. i., p. 138.

he took his fellowship. At Oxford he had much personal influence, but his labours there seemed to have borne but little permanent fruit. He had left no ' school of the prophets ' behind him at the University. His career in Georgia had been an almost ignominious failure. His bitter confessions, written during the voyage home, and immediately after his return, are well known. ' One thing I have learnt in the ends of the earth, that I who went to America to convert the Indians was never converted myself.'

Wesley himself, in after-life, took a less severe view of his own case and character at this period. He would hardly, in 1770, have maintained, as he affirmed in 1738, that he was an unconverted man during all the time he was in Georgia. But to his life's end he held that he was in many and important respects an unenlightened man, and that he was wanting in that filial and evangelical faith and in that spiritual power which belong to the character and experience of a Christian in the highest sense of the word. Nor is it possible to understand in the least his after-life, unless it be apprehended that in 1738 a vital and critical change passed on his experience, and one which transformed, in many ways, his character for all his following course.

Already, before he had landed at Deal on
February 1st, 1738, he had definitively adopted
the doctrine of ' salvation by faith.' In this
respect, his voyage home, with his unbroken
and solitary reflections on all that he had seen
and learnt during the two years which had
passed since his leaving England, seems to
have borne decisive fruit. But until he met
with Böhler—which, however, was very soon
after he landed,—he still regarded faith as
largely a question of creeds and of the in-
tellect. Böhler taught, on the contrary, that
faith was critically and essentially a moral act
and habit of the heart and soul, exercised
through the help of the Divine Spirit, and
bearing no necessary *ratio* or relation whatever to the *quantum* of a man's creed, or to
any intellectual process or attainment. Having
once accepted this doctrine, Wesley never
afterwards forgot it.

I know of no writer who has shown more
insight in dealing with this part of Wesley's
history than Miss Wedgwood. It is remarkable that, standing distinctly apart from the
theology of Wesley, she has yet appreciated
so justly the spiritual *momenta* of his development as a man of faith and power.

' Wesley's homeward voyage in 1738,' says Miss
Wedgwood, ' marks the conclusion of his High Church

period. He abated nothing of his attachment to the ordinances of the Church, either then or to the last day of his life; and he did not so soon reach that degree of independence of her hierarchy and some of her rules which marks his farthest point of divergence; but his journals during this voyage chronicle for us that deep dissatisfaction which is felt wherever an earnest nature wakes up to the incompleteness of a traditional religion; and his after-life, compared with his two years in Georgia, makes it evident that he passed at this time into a new spiritual region. . . . "By Peter Böhler, in the hand of the great God," he writes in his journal, "I was, on March 5th, fully convinced of the want of that faith whereby we are saved." . . . But the reader cannot but ask, What is the meaning of this conversion? No candid person can read the account of Wesley's life before and after the change he so described and doubt that something did really happen then. . . . It is the most memorable of all events when any one wakes up to the conviction that besides all the men and women he sees round about him there is a Person who is not seen, but who is just as real as they, and an agent in a sense in which they are not; when he comes to feel that certain results are due to the will of God, not only in the sense in which any one must believe in it who believes in Him at all—that He is almighty, and could prevent it if He chose—but in that same direct, personal sense in which a man's lifting his hand is the result of his choosing to do so. It is literally and simply a new life. An element is come into the man's dealings with his fellow-men which alters everything, and which, in the words of one who will always be remembered among the best exponents of this change (St. Augustine), makes it delightful to escape from that which before it was unendurable to give up, and impossible to avoid that which it was before impossible to do. . . . The witness that the direct influence of God upon the spirit of man was not confined to a remote past or a mysterious future, but was an actual fact in the lives of all who truly deserved the name of Christian, came home to Wesley and to many others of that day as the one force that was to bind a society together and to give new life to the individual soul. . . . The birthday of a Christian was shifted from his baptism to his conversion, and in that change the partition line of two great systems is crossed.'

Such is Miss Wedgwood's philosophical explanation, in general terms, of what took place at this crisis of Wesley's life. Wesleyans say—as Wesley himself would have said—that the explanation is so vague and general as to be essentially defective. There is not a word here of that deep sense and conviction of sin and helplessness which lay at the root of Wesley's conversion; nothing of the atoning work of Christ. Nevertheless, it is true as far as it goes; and it marks very justly the critical character of the change, of the ' conversion,' through which Wesley now passed.

At the first with Wesley, as with most men of that age, faith had meant the intellectual acceptance of the creeds, together with the submission of the will to the laws and services of the Church. Of course, after 1730, when his attention had been directed to the rubrics and to the teachings of tradition, his faith, thus regarded, included in its scope much more of ecclesiastical observance than it did at an earlier period. Presently, to the two elements I have noted was added a third, that, viz., of intense contemplation with a view to realise the mystical union of the soul with God. This latter element, it must be observed was theosophical, not evangelical. In Georgia, however, the mystical ideas of contemplative union with God began to give place to the thought of spiritual union with Jesus Christ. Mysticism faded away by degrees—he himself says he could hardly tell how—and evangelical ideas and desires took possession of him instead. This grew and deepened during his voyage home. Still, until he met with Böhler, he had not embraced, scarcely, it would seem, had conceived, the idea of faith as being, in its main element, personal trust and self-surrender, as having for its central object the atonement of Jesus Christ, and as inspired and sustained by the supernatural aid and concurrence of the Holy Spirit. As yet faith in his view was a union of intellectual belief and of voluntary self-submission, acted out day by day, and hour after hour, in all the moralities of ordinary life, and in all the prescribed means and services of the Church, Christ being held in view as the Saviour of the race, and as the Exemplar for all men. From this conception of faith the element of the supernatural was wanting, and equally that of personal trust for salvation on the atonement of Jesus Christ.

Now, the work of Peter Böhler was to convince Wesley that such faith as this was, after all, but a man's own work, the result of his own logic and will, and not in any sense the true vital faith of a Christian. Wesley, after many days of close controversy, was at length convinced that the Moravian was right. 'Mi frater, mi frater,' said Böhler, 'ista philosophia tua excoquenda est.' It was no easy matter to accomplish this task; but once effected, it seems to have been done for ever. Wesley confessed that Böhler's teaching was true Gospel teaching. He now believed himself for the first time to understand the words of St. Paul, when he said, 'I am crucified with Christ: nevertheless I live; yet not I, but Christ liveth in me, and the life which I now live in the flesh I live by the faith of the Son of God, who loved me, and gave Himself for me.' Such faith as this, and such only, he conceived could be said to be 'faith of the operation of the Holy Ghost.' Such faith he some years later described as 'the loving, obedient sight of a present and reconciled God.' He believed himself now to understand for the first time the meaning of the apostle when he speaks of the inward kingdom of God as 'righteousness and peace, and joy in the Holy Ghost.'

If I have seemed somewhat to labour this point, it is because it is simply impossible to understand either Wesley's character or his course without understanding the critical and vital change which at this time passed upon him. Here ended really his High Church stage of life. Here began his life as an evangelist and a Church revivalist. All dates from his final and decisive acceptance of Böhler's teaching as to the nature of faith, and from that which followed on the 24th day of May, as described in his own words, when he 'felt his heart strangely warmed ; felt that he did trust in Christ, Christ alone for salvation,' and had 'an assurance given him that Christ had taken away his sin, and saved him from the law of sin and death.' *

* This 'assurance' was what Wesley, in his mature and settled theology, spoke of as the 'Witness of the Spirit.' It was an inward persuasion of present accept- ance and favour ; but, unlike the Calvinistic 'assur- ance,' had no distinct reference to the final perseverance and acceptance of the believer. It was not for some years that Wesley's views as to the 'Witness of the Spirit,' its meaning, and its relations became definite

From this time forth Wesley was no longer characteristically a priest; his vocation was pre-eminently that of a preacher. He was never again to be a settled pastor; he was henceforth to be an itinerant evangelist. Though for some time yet he retained his rubrical scruples and punctilios as to the necessity of episcopalian baptism, and even went so far, on at least one occasion, contrary

and settled. Moravian statements of experience seem at first to have left him in much perplexity. Here, in a note, I may refer to another specially Wesleyan doctrine, which it is beside my plan to discuss or analyse in the text—what Wesley was accustomed to speak of as 'Christian perfection,' or 'perfect love.' Wesley did not at all mean 'sinless perfection.' But his analysis of human nature seems to have been metaphysically inadequate; and for this, as well as other reasons, his statements of this doctrine often appear to be vague, if not sometimes inconsistent. There has always been some difference of view among Methodists, both as to the precise nature of Christian perfection and the manner or the stages of its attainment. John and Charles Wesley, indeed, did not always agree on the matter. In the main, however, this Wesleyan tenet must be regarded as a protest against extreme Calvinistic views, amounting sometimes to gross antinomian perversions, on the subject of 'imputed righteousness' and indwelling and abiding sin. A catena of eminent writers, beginning with Clement of Alexandria, and including both saintly Catholics and high mystics of different nations, have built on the teaching of St. John and St. Paul an exalted doctrine of Christian perfection.

to the counsel of the Bishop of London, as to re-baptize Dissenters, yet henceforth the sacraments, according to his teaching, were to be regarded only as means and seals of grace, not as fountains of supernatural power, ministered by the hand of the priest.

It is remarkable, indeed, how very little is found on the subject of baptism in the fourteen volumes of Wesley's works. He revised and re-issued, under his own name, in 1756, the treatise on that subject which his father had published more than half a century before, and which teaches 'baptismal regeneration' after the mildest type of the doctrine, and much as it had been taught by the Puritan divines of the Church of England. Elsewhere all that Wesley says on the subject, besides two sentences in his *Notes on the New Testament,* to which I refer in a note below, is in two sermons, and in his *Farther Appeal to Men of Reason and Religion,* and amounts altogether to but a few lines. He allows that infants are made children of God in baptism. 'It is certain,' he says, 'our Church supposes that all who are baptized in their infancy are at the same time born again ; and it is allowed that the whole office for the baptism of infants proceeds upon this supposition.' 'But yet,' he insists, 'there may be the outward sign,

where there is not the inward grace.' 'Whatever be the case with infants, it is sure all
of riper years who are baptized are not at
the same time born again.' * These words
occur in the sermon on the 'New Birth.'
In his sermon on 'The Marks of the New
Birth' he only refers to the subject at all
in order to rebut the pretensions of those who
claimed to be Christians on the strength of
their baptism when infants. He allows that
as infants they were regenerated, but asks
vehemently and repeatedly of what avail that
fact can be in the case of those who are now
beyond question living godless and wicked
lives. In the *Farther Appeal* he uses precisely equivalent, almost identical, language
in one place, † while in another he says that
'Our Church supposes infants to be *justified*

---

* In his *Notes on the New Testament*, which volume
is not included in the general edition of his *Works*, but
is sold separately, Wesley thus expresses himself as to
the point touched in the passage quoted in the text.
Writing on Acts xxii. 16, he says, speaking of adults,
it must be remembered: 'Baptism administered to
real penitents is both a means and seal of pardon.
Nor did God ordinarily, *in the primitive Church*, bestow
this on any except through this means.' Compare also
the note on John iii. 5. It cannot be said that there
is any necessary contrariety between what I have now
quoted, and the passage quoted in the text.

† *Works*, viii., p. 48.

in baptism, although they cannot then either believe or repent.'* Higher than this John Wesley's baptismal doctrine never went, so far as his writings show. The most remarkable thing, indeed, in regard to Wesley's teaching on baptism, is his reticence. Many, probably most, of his preachers no less than of his people, during his lifetime rejected altogether the doctrine of baptismal regeneration, and he never required any of them to receive it. He made no sign except to republish the treatise to which I have referred, and to make the brief and merely incidental references to the subject which I have noted in two of his sermons. To this day Wesleyan Methodism remains destitute of any explicit doctrine on the subject of baptismal grace. There are still, I believe, a few Wesleyan ministers who receive the doctrine of baptismal regeneration. There are probably many more who believe in what Wesley and his father spoke of as a 'principle of grace' imparted to the soul of the infant in baptism ; but there can be no doubt that the prevalent conviction within the 'Connexion' is strongly against the doctrine of baptismal regeneration. I imagine that the variety and general balance of opinion on this subject in modern Meth-

* Ibid, p. 52.

odism are not very different from what existed
in early Methodism after the Connexion was
fully and widely organised. What is very
remarkable is, that Wesley made no effort to
convert his people to his own opinions. Indeed, it has been contended, not without considerable show of reason, that Wesley must,
in his later years, have ceased to hold, or at
least have come to doubt of, the doctrine of
baptismal regeneration. In 1784 he prepared
and published, originally for the use of the
offshoot Methodist Church in America, *The
Sunday Service of the Methodists, with other
Occasional Services,* a volume which still holds
an authorised and honoured place among
Methodist formularies, although the abridged
Sunday service here given is seldom pre-
ferred by Wesleyans to the full Church Service in English Wesleyan chapels where the
Liturgy is in use. In this volume are contained, instead of the Thirty-nine Articles,
twenty-five Articles of Religion, which are
now the authoritative standard of the largest
Protestant Church in the world—the Methodist
Episcopal Church of the United States.
These articles are for the most part substantially the same, or nearly so, with those of
the thirty-nine to which they correspond.
In some cases, however, they are materially

abridged. This is the case in particular with that which relates to baptism, in which all that is taught as to the nature of baptism is, that, besides being a sign of the Christian profession, it is ' also a sign of regeneration or the new birth.' As to baptism as an instrument, as to the effects of baptism, not a word is said. This article proves, at all events, that Wesley had in 1784 concluded not to insist on the doctrine of baptismal regeneration in any sense. *

As to the Lord's Supper the case is still plainer. Here he has in various places clearly and fully expressed his views, and those views were certainly not what would in the present day be regarded as High Church. It appears, indeed, as I have already noted, to be more than doubtful whether, although he always to his latest day insisted on frequent communion — indeed, on ' constant communion,' that is, communion at every opportunity—he at any time of his life held really high doctrine as to the Lord's Supper. In 1788 he published a sermon which he had

* *The Sunday Service of the Methodists.* Three editions were published by Mr. Wesley, one in 1784 for America, and two afterwards for this country (1786 and 1788). [The articles are also contained in the complete and revised Service Book of the Wesleyan Methodists published in 1883].

written at Oxford, 'for the use of his pupils,' fifty-five years before—that is, in 1733—when he carried to the utmost his rubrical Anglicanism at the University. He says, in the brief preface to this publication, 'I have added very little, but retrenched much, as I then used more words than I do now. But I thank God I have not yet seen cause to alter my sentiments in any point which is therein delivered.' The only phrase in the sermon which looks like high sacramental doctrine is one in which he speaks of the Lord's Supper as the 'Christian sacrifice.' But that he uses this phrase in a merely figurative sense is certain and evident from the explicit statements which precede and follow. He says : 'As our bodies are strengthened by bread and wine, so are our souls by these tokens of the body and blood of Christ.' 'The design of this Sacrament is, the continual remembrance of the death of Christ by eating bread and drinking wine, which are the outward signs of the inward grace, the body and blood of Christ.' 'As the apostles were obliged to bless, break, and give the bread to all that joined with them in these holy things, so were all Christians obliged to receive those signs of Christ's body and blood. Here, therefore, the bread and wine are commanded to be received in remembrance of His death to the end of the world.'

There are distinct indications that at the time John Wesley published this old Oxford sermon he was, in different ways, returning in his extreme old age (84—85) to the love of his youth. His brother Charles, whose strong Anglican bias had obliged Wesley to lean to the other side, in order to hold the balance safely and wisely with his preachers, had been some years dead ; his anti-Church of England preachers—he had many such—respected his great age, and waited for his death to assert their own ideas and claims; his enemies, on all sides round, were now at peace with him ; he was no longer proscribed or attacked by any section of the clergy, but was publicly honoured by very many, including men of the highest distinction ; and he was not altogether superior to the fond clingings and idolatries of age, which lead men to look back so lovingly to the memories and affections of their youth. Hence he became in the last few years of his life more Anglican in his feelings than he had been at perhaps any time since his conversion. And yet he came no nearer to high Anglican doctrine as to the real presence, as to sacramental mysteries and efficacy, than may be understood from the foregoing quotations.

The sermon from which I have quoted is not included among the standard sermons which all Methodist preachers are required to read and to accept, as containing the general system of Methodist theology. All he says on the subject in his standard sermons is contained in the one on 'The Means of Grace,' and is altogether contrary to the teaching of modern sacramentarian 'Anglo-Catholics.' ' "He said, Take, eat : this is My body "—that is, the sacred sign of My body.'   ' " He took the cup, saying, This cup is the new testament " or covenant, " in My blood " : the sacred sign of that covenant.'   ' " As oft as ye eat this bread, and drink this cup, ye do show forth the Lord's death till He come " : ye openly exhibit the same by these visible signs ; ye manifest your solemn remembrance of His death, till He cometh in the clouds of heaven.'

There is other evidence of Wesley's doctrine on this subject, which, though indirect, is yet decisive, and in entire harmony with what has thus far been before us.   He sanctioned in his middle-age the publication of extracts from Dr. Brevint's tractate on *The Christian Sacrament and Sacrifice*, as a preface to his brother Charles' *Hymns on the Lord's Supper.* 'The Lord's Supper,' Dr. Brevint teaches,

E

' was chiefly ordained for a sacrament (1) to *represent* the sufferings of Christ which are *past,* whereof it is a *memorial;* (2) to *convey* the first fruits of these sufferings in *present graces,* whereof it is a *means;* and (3) to assure us of glory to come, whereof it is an infallible *pledge.*' And, as to the crucial point, on the second of these heads he thus explains himself more precisely: ' His body and blood have *everywhere,* but especially at this Sacrament, *a true and real presence. . . . * Since *He is gone up, He sends down to earth the graces* that spring continually both from His everlasting sacrifice, and from the continual intercession that attends it.'* Perhaps it might be inferred from the last passage cited that Dr. Brevint believed in the Lutheran dogma of the ubiquity of our Lord's bodily presence. But it is evident that he did not believe in the real corporeal presence of our Lord in and under the elements of bread and wine, in virtue of the priestly consecration. Brevint's doctrine Charles Wesley transfused into ecstatic hymns, which are full of the 'real presence' indeed, but contain no trace of any doctrine equivalent to the modern High ' Catholic' teaching as to the corporeal

---

**The Poetical Works of J. and C. Wesley,* vol. iii., pp. 186, 197.

presence of the incarnate Christ in the consecrated bread and wine of the Eucharist.

It seems evident, accordingly, that however extreme may have been Wesley's High
Churchmanship at Oxford, he held no high
Anglo-Catholic tenets as to the sacraments during his after life. It is indeed more than doubtful whether, on the subject of the Eucharist at
least, he had at any time held doctrine which
would now be regarded as high. At Oxford
he was full of devotional ritualism ; he had a
great reverence also for primitive symbolism
and for ancient tradition generally, and accordingly at one time would have the sacramental
wine mixed with water. He insisted strongly
on baptism, as he did on every rubrical requirement, however minute or punctilious.
As a loyal and obedient Churchman he conceived himself bound by his ordination vows
to make a conscience of all these matters.
He laid great stress on ' constant communion,'
and on full and close preparation for such communion, including a private visit to the minister. But he did not even in Oxford believe
in any such doctrine as that of the supernatural bodily presence of the Lord Jesus in
the consecrated elements, as now taught by
advanced High Churchmen.

CHAPTER III.

THE REVOLUTION IN WESLEY'S ECCLESIAS-
TICAL VIEWS AFTER HIS CONVERSION.

SOME REMAINS OF HIGH CHURCH PRINCIPLES FOR
SEVERAL YEARS—RITUALISM AND HIERARCHICAL
SUPERSTITION FINALLY RENOUNCED AND ABAN-
DONED—HIS CHURCHMANSHIP MUCH MORE
BROAD THAN HIGH.

FOR many months before Wesley's 'conversion'— in Georgia, on the voyage
home, and in the interval after his return—a
process of undermining had been going on,
which had left his system of High Church
habits and observances almost without a
foundation. After his conversion, the undermined fabric fell into manifest ruins, although
some fragments of it were left standing for
several years afterwards. What passed immediately after his conversion between himself
and his friends the Huttons is very significant,
although it must be remembered that the
Huttons are the narrators, and may perhaps
have represented what took place more sharply
and startlingly than it would appear if we
possessed Wesley's own account. Mr. Hutton,
let me explain, was a retired clergyman, who
had been long a particular friend of the Wesley

brothers, having been intimate with Samuel
Wesley when he was one of the masters at
Westminster School, and his near neighbour.
Mr. Hutton's house was in College Street,
Westminster. Here, a few days after Wesley's
' conversion '—the hour, that is, when, as he
himself describes it, his heart was ' strangely
warmed,' and he found rest and peace through
faith in Christ for salvation—Mr. Hutton was
reading to a company in his study a sermon
of Bishop Blackall's, when Wesley stood up
and told those present that five days before
he was not a Christian. ' Mr. Hutton,' to
quote Mr. Tyerman's account, ' was thunder-
struck, and said, "Have a care, Mr. Wesley,
how you despise the benefits received by the
two sacraments"; Wesley afterwards repeated
his declaration, upon which Mrs. Hutton
answered, "If you have not been a Christian
ever since I knew you, you have been a great
hypocrite, for you made us all believe that you
were one." To this Wesley rejoined, "When
we renounce everything but faith and get into
Christ, then, and not till then, have we any
reason to believe that we are Christians." '

The language Wesley used may have been
crude or unguarded, or perhaps only an im-
perfect account of it may here be given, but
there can be no reasonable doubt as to the sub-

stantial accuracy of this relation nor as to its
meaning. To Wesley's transformed apprehen-
sion, as Miss Wedgwood says, in words already
quoted, 'the birthday of a Christian was
shifted from his baptism to his conversion, and
in that change the partition line of two great
systems is crossed.' The date of Wesley's
Christian birthday, according to this reckon-
ing, was, as we have noted, May 24th, 1738.
Let that date be well marked. Wesley's inner
and essential ultra-High-Churchmanship belongs to the period preceding this date. Then
follows a transition period, during which he
was gradually getting rid of his high ecclesiastical tenets and prejudices, and which came to
its complete end in 1745–6. After this period
he may have been in a certain sense a High
Churchman—it is certain he was never a Low
Churchman in the modern sense, he was indeed rather broad than low—but his High
Churchmanship in after-life, and through the
space of nearly half a century, included neither
high sacramentarian doctrine nor servile vener-
ation for rubrics, nor any belief in either the
virtue or the reality of what is commonly
called ' the apostolical succession.'

Wesley's conversion took place at a religious fellowship-meeting, held in Aldersgate
Street, connected with one of those societies

organised within the Church of England, with which the names of Dr. Horneck and Dr. Woodward are associated, and the propriety and special value of which had been defended so vigorously by his own father forty years before. It was while one was reading Luther's preface to the Epistle to the Romans that the critical change took place. It is no wonder that fellowship meetings henceforth were inseparable from the spiritual life of the Wesleys.

'When Wesley returned from America,' says Miss Wedgwood, 'these societies formed a natural organisation for one who desired fellowship in a religious body more developed and coherent than the Church of England, and it was in these societies that all the chief peculiarities of Methodism took their rise. The Methodist class-meeting was no more than "the weekly conference among young communicants" recommended by the earlier body, thereby to "admonish and watch over one another, and to fortify each other against those temptations which assault them from the world and their own corruptions" (Dr. Woodward's Account, p. 75). "And these persons, knowing each other's manner of life and their particular frailties and temptations, partly by their familiar conversation, and partly from their own inward experience, can much better inspect, admonish, and guard each other than the most careful minister usually can." Here we have an exact description of a Methodist class-meeting, written about four years before Wesley was born (1699). Like the early Methodists, too, the religious societies were distinguished by their frequent communion, and the reverence paid by them to this rite;

they had also their charitable fund, and their stewards
elected yearly.'

These earlier societies, however, were, as
Miss Wedgwood proceeds to say, distinctively
Church societies. Their spirit and tone were
in conformity with the views and feelings of
the Wesleys before they had embraced Peter
Böhler's teaching as to the 'righteousness of
faith.' Orthodoxy, the instituted means of
grace, and beneficence—summed up for these
societies all that appertained to the Christian
character and profession. Of the 'new heart'
and the 'new life' their members knew nothing. 'The spirit of the older societies,' as
Miss Wedgwood says, 'was not only unlike
that of Methodism, it was the very spirit from
which Methodism was a reaction.' Hence
the ideas and experience of the Wesleys after
they had become disciples of their Moravian
teacher were to these societies as new wine
to old bottles. Some of the members, no
doubt, followed the Wesleys and became par-
takers of the like experience. But many
were filled with alarm and dismay. It was
probably at a meeting of one of these societies
that Wesley, at Mr. Hutton's house, startled
his host and hostess in the manner which has
been described.

Wesley did not at once, perhaps never did

formally, separate himself from these Church of England societies. From many of them he was before long excluded ; of that there can be no doubt. There was, however, one society, which early in 1738 he and his brother took part in establishing, though they only ranked as private members in it, and which met in Fetter Lane, of which Wesley was accustomed to speak as ' our society.' With this for two years Wesley was closely identified, the society consisting exclusively of members of the Church of England. Although nominally but private members there can be no doubt that Wesley and his brother Charles were in reality the leaders of this society, and had for a long time a settled ascendency in it. Under their guidance, the society was organised somewhat closely on the Moravian model. Their influence, however, was in 1740 undermined by the Moravian teachers, Molther and Spangenberg, whose worse than foolish vagaries— their mystical quietism and doctrinal antinomianism—fascinated and bewildered many of the members. The consequence was that, after long forbearance, Wesley and his brother separated themselves in 1740 from this society, carrying with them their own adherents—a minority—to the Foundery, Moorfields, where he had already in the preceding year organised a society of his own, with which the faithful remnant who accompanied the Wesleys from Fetter Lane were now united.

The Foundery was an old place which he had a short while before secured for his own use, and had repaired and fitted up for the purpose of religious meetings. Here was the real beginning of Wesleyan Methodism, as an organised system. The private fellowship-meeting—a little later organised systematically as a class-meeting—was its nucleus, its 'germ cell,' as it has been truly called by Wesleyan writers.

Such meetings as these, however, could be of little avail apart from the work of preaching. Preaching, indeed, was the characteristic force of the new movement of which the Wesleys had become chief lights and leaders. Whitefield had already given evidence of this. Himself formerly one of Wesley's Oxford pupils and religious disciples, he had, as all men know, embraced the doctrines of evangelical faith and 'experimental religion,' and had passed into the enjoyment of the ' new life' before either of the brothers. As an immediate consequence he had become a preacher —a preacher of extraordinary power and unbounded popularity. He, however, was in America during the early months which followed the conversion of the brothers. Now, having passed through a similar experience to that of Whitefield, the Wesleys, like him, had become preachers. In popularity they presently became the rivals of Whitefield, while as respects decisive and permanent results, John Wesley's power as a preacher was even superior to that of Whitefield.*

In all that I have now described we see evidences of the essential change in ecclesiastical bias which had passed upon Wesley. Henceforth his dominant tendency was altogether different from what it had been before. His face was now set in an opposite direction.

Wesleyan writers take their stand here. None have shown so distinctly and fully the rigid and excessive Churchmanship of Wesley up to the date of 1738. But they insist that, from that date, everything was essentially different, and that the essential difference very swiftly developed into striking results.

The High Churchman, they argue, makes salvation to be directly dependent on sacramental grace and apostolical succession. Whereas the evangelical believer, the man who has received the doctrine of salvation by faith, as it was taught by Peter Böhler, and

---

*I may be allowed here to refer to the chapter on 'Wesley the Preacher,' in my *Living Wesley.*

as it is understood by the Reformed Churches
in general, learns from St. Paul that 'faith
cometh by hearing, and hearing by the Word
of God.' Hence, according to his conviction,
the Christian salvation—justification, regeneration, and sanctification—must be realised by
means of the 'truth as it is in Jesus.' Truth
and life are for him indissolubly associated.
He cannot forget the words of the Word Himself, ' Sanctify them through Thy Truth ; Thy
word is Truth ' ; and again, ' I am the Way,
the Truth, and the Life ' ; nor the words of
St. Paul, when he speaks of himself and his
fellow-workers as ' by manifestation of the
truth commending themselves to every man's
conscience in the sight of God.' It is the
truth in the sacraments, according to his view,
which fills them with blessing to those who
receive them with faith ; they are ' signs and
seals,' eloquent symbols and most sacred
pledges ; but they are not, in and of themselves, saturated with grace and life ; they are
not the only organs and vehicles through
which grace flows to the members of Christ's
mystical body, nor is their efficacy, irrespective
of any divine truth, apprehended and embraced
by the mind and heart of the believer.

Wesleyans admit that, up to 1738, Wesley
had been a High Church Ritualist, but they

insist that all his life afterwards he taught the evangelical doctrine of salvation by faith ; that before long, and once for all, he discarded the fable,' as he called it, of 'apostolical succession,' and that he presently gave up all that is now understood to belong to the system, whether theological or ecclesiastical, of High Church Anglo-Catholicism. 'The grave-clothes of ritualistic superstition,' they say, ' still hung about him for a while, even after he had come forth from the sepulchre, and had, in his heart and soul, been set loose and free ; and he only cast them off gradually. But the new principle he had embraced led,' as they affirm, ' before long to his complete emancipation from the principles and prejudices of High Church ecclesiasticism.'

Such language as this may seem to High Churchmen harsh, and perhaps uncharitable, but the one question really is, how far it is warranted by the history and the recorded sentiments of Wesley himself after the year 1738. Modern Wesleyans cannot be expected to be more High Church than their founder. I propose, accordingly, to show now in some detail what Wesley did actually claim and hold as to matters ecclesiastical during the half-century which followed his ' conversion.' Ecclesiastical claims and theories are founded on theological dogmas. We shall see how the newly-received doctrines of grace and of faith gave colour and form to the ecclesiastical principles of the founder of Methodism.

It is hard to conceive views as to the public ministry of the word, and the government and discipline of the Church, more hazardous and untenable, according to the standard of High Churchmen, than those which were maintained by John Wesley.

He held, as I will presently show, after the year 1745, that, the office of presbyter or priest and that of bishop being originally and essentially one, he, as a presbyter, had the abstract and essential right to ordain presbyters, in a new sphere—a sphere of his own creation, so to speak—if by his so doing neither he nor they whom he ordained became intruders into other communions, or trespassers within other jurisdictions. Acting on this principle, he ordained ' presbyters,' and even ' superintendents ' * or bishops, for America ; he ordained presbyters for Scotland ; and

* In Wesley's time, the senior preacher in charge was called 'assistant,' not as now 'superintendent.' The preachers generally were called 'helpers.' ' Superintendent,' in Wesley's ecclesiastical nomenclature, meant 'bishop'; he held, of course, that his ' superintendents,' or ' bishops,' were not in order, but only in office, distinguished from presbyters.

eventually felt himself constrained and even driven to ordain presbyters to assist him in administering the sacraments to his own societies in England, one of his strong pleas being that the clergy in many instances would not admit his people to the Lord's Supper. Indeed there is high authority—the authority of Samuel Bradburn, one of his ablest and most eminent preachers—for saying that Wesley went so far, at the Conference of 1788, as to consecrate one of his English preachers as 'superintendent,' or bishop. The Methodist Conference did but extend this principle to its obvious consequences when, a few years after his death, those of them whom Wesley had already ordained were presumed to have the power to share their prerogatives with their brethren and partners in common charge of the societies, so that all the societies which desired it might receive the sacraments from their own preachers.

Quite as radical, indeed, as any opinion of a modern Methodist on these points, and far more startling, as coming from John Wesley, is the following passage contained in the Minutes of Conference for the year already noted, 1745 :—

'*Q.* 1.—Can he be a spiritual governor of the Church who is not a believer nor a member of it ?

'*A.*—It seems not : though he may be a governor in outward things by a power derived from the King.

'*Q.* 2.—What are properly the laws of the Church of England?

'*A.*—The rubrics; and to those we submit as the ordinance of man, for the Lord's sake.

'*Q.* 3.—But is not the will of our governors a law?

'*A.*—No; not of any governor, temporal or spiritual. Therefore, if any bishop wills that I should not preach the Gospel, his will is no law to me.

'*Q.* 4.—But what if he produce a law against your preaching?

'*A.*—I am to obey God rather than man.

'*Q.* 5.—Is Episcopal, Presbyterian, or Independent church government most agreeable to reason?

'*A.*—The plain origin of church government seems to be this. Christ sends forth a preacher of the Gospel. Some who hear him repent and believe the Gospel. They then desire him to watch over them, to build them up in the faith, and to guide their souls in the paths of righteousness.

'Here, then, is an *Independent* congregation subject to no pastor but their own; neither liable to be controlled in things spiritual by any other man or body of men whatsoever.

'But soon after, some from other parts, who are occasionally present while he speaks in the name of Him that sent him, beseech him to come over to help them also. Knowing it to be the will of God, he consents, yet not till he has conferred with the wisest and holiest of his congregation, and, with their advice, appointed one or more who have gifts and grace to watch over the flock till his return.

'If it pleases God to raise another flock in the new place, before he leaves them he does the same thing, appointing one whom God has fitted for the work to watch over these souls also. In like manner, in every place where it pleases God to gather a little flock by His Word, he appoints one in his absence to take the oversight of the rest, and to assist them of the abilities which God giveth. These are *deacons*, or servants of the church, and look on the first pastor as their common father. And all these congregations regard him in the same light, and esteem him still as the shepherd of their souls.

' These congregations are not absolutely *independent;* they depend on one pastor, though not on each other.

' As these congregations increase, and as their deacons grow in years and grace, they need other subordinate deacons or helpers, in respect of whom they may be called *presbyters* or elders, as their father in the Lord may be called the bishop or overseer of them all.

' *Q.* 6.—Is mutual consent absolutely necessary between the pastor and his flock ?

' *A.*—No question. I cannot guide any soul unless he consent to be guided by me. Neither can any soul force me to guide him if I consent not.

' *Q.* 7.—Does the ceasing of this consent on either side dissolve that relation ?

' *A.*—It must, in the very nature of things. If a man no longer consent to be guided by me, I am no longer his guide : I am free. If one will not guide me any longer, I am free to seek one who will.' *

This remarkable extract contains implicitly the whole theory of Methodist government and discipline, regarded as an organisation created and controlled by Wesley for the pur-

* *Minutes of Conference,* vol. i., pp. 26, 27. Last edition.

pose of converting souls and of watching over his converts. Wesley regarded himself as a sort of bishop, his ' assistants ' or chief preachers in charge as quasi-presbyters, and the junior or probationary ' helpers ' as a sort of deacons. If he never carried out this conception thoroughly in practice, and especially never conceded to his chief preachers generally the distinct status of presbyters, it was because he cherished, more or less, though with heavy doubts and misgivings, the hope that the bishops of his Church might be brought to give virtual effect to his desires, and that Methodism might become an affiliated branch of the Church of England.

It is true, indeed, and it is very singular, that even at the time he penned the remarkable extract just given, Wesley still retained some considerable relics of his ecclesiastical High Churchmanship. The date of the minute is August, 1745. On December 27th of the same year he prints in his journal a letter to his brother-in-law, Hall—a letter well known and often quoted by Churchmen—in which he upholds the doctrines of apostolical succession, and of the threefold order of the ministry. On the very next page of his journal, however, under date January 20th, 1746—and no doubt the juxtaposition was calculated and intended by the journalist—he declares and publishes his definitive renunciation of these selfsame views, as the result of reading Lord (Chancellor) King's *Account of the Primitive Church*. From this conclusion he never afterwards swerved. In a letter to his brother Charles many years afterwards (1785) he spoke of ' the uninterrupted succession ' as ' knowing it to be a fable, which no man ever did or can prove.' *

During his subsequent course he more than once speaks of himself as ' a Scriptural Episcopos '; and, as we have seen, he acted on this persuasion.†

In the *Disciplinary Minutes* for 1746‡ it is said that the Wesleys and their helpers may ' perhaps be regarded as extraordinary messengers, designed of God to provoke the others to jealousy.' The following suggestive question and answer are also given in the same Minutes. ' Why do we not use more form and solemnity in the receiving of a new labourer ?—We purposely decline it : first, because there is something of stateliness in

---

* Jackson's *Life of Charles Wesley*, vol. ii., p. 395. Twenty-four years before this, in 1761, he had said the same thing in a letter to the *London Chronicle*, in reply to a tract entitled, *A Caveat against the Methodists,—Works*, iii., p. 42 (*Journal*, February 13—20, 1761).

† *Works*, vol. xiii., pp. 240, 257.

‡ *Minutes*, vol. i., pp. 30, 31.

it; second, because we would not make haste.
We desire barely to follow Providence as it
gradually opens.' The Minutes for 1747 contain the following decisive series of questions
and answers :—

'*Q.* 6.—Does a church in the New Testament always
mean a single congregation ?

'*A.*—We believe it does. We do not recollect any
instance to the contrary.

'*Q.* 7.—What instance or ground is there then in
the New Testament for a *National* Church ?

'*A.*—We know none at all. We apprehend it to be
a merely political institution.

'*Q.* 8.—Are the three orders of bishops, priests, and
deacons plainly described in the New Testament ?

'*A.*—We think they are ; and believe they generally
obtained in the churches of the apostolic age.

'*Q.* 9.—But are you assured that God designed the same
plan should obtain in all churches throughout all ages ?

'*A.*—We are not assured of this; because we do
not know that it is asserted in Holy Writ.

'*Q.* 10.—If this plan were essential to a Christian
church, what would become of all the foreign Reformed
Churches ?

'*A.*—It would follow they are no parts of the Church
of Christ ; a consequence full of shocking absurdity.

'*Q.* 11.—In what age was the divine right of Episcopacy first asserted in England ?

'*A.*—About the middle of Queen Elizabeth's reign.
Till then, all the bishops and clergy in England continually allowed and joined in the ministration of those
who were not episcopally ordained.

'*Q.* 12.—Must there not be numberless accidental
varieties in the government of various churches ?

' *A.*—There must, in the nature of things. For as God variously dispenses His gifts of nature, providence, and grace, both the offices themselves and the officers in each ought to be varied from time to time.

' *Q.* 13.—Why is it that there is no determinate plan of church government appointed in Scripture ?

' *A.*—Without doubt, because the wisdom of God had a regard to this necessary variety.

' *Q.* 14.—Was there any thought of uniformity in the government of all churches until the time of Constantine ?

' *A.*—It is certain there was not, and would not have been then had men consulted the Word of God only.'*

So far Wesley had travelled since 1738, so thoroughly different were his views in 1747 from what they had been in 1735. So profound was the contradiction between the principles of the Oxford Methodist and of the founder of the Methodist Connexion of societies. The former was a priest and pastor among 'the schools of the prophets,' devoted to the rubrics and order of his Church ; the latter was an itinerant evangelist for his nation and the world, loving his National Church indeed, but regarding it as a ' political institution,' and always prepared to sacrifice, if it were necessary, his Churchmanship to what he regarded as his higher and wider mission as a preacher and teacher of the Gospel to all men. Nearly forty years later, in 1785, in the

* *Minutes,* vol. i., p. 36. Last Edition.

letter to his brother Charles, lately referred
to, Wesley reaffirms all that he had said in
the *Minutes* I have quoted, and even speaks
more decisively as to the definition and character of the National Church.* He uses language, besides, as to the existing Church, of
singular trenchancy. He quotes, as descrip-
tive of the priesthood of the Church of England, a line from one of Charles' own poems—

'Heathenish priests and mitred infidels':

in regard to which line I may say, further, that
in a letter dated three weeks later he says,
'Your verse is a sad truth. I see fifty times
more of England than you do, and I find few
exceptions to it.' He declares, as to the ' "uninterrupted succession," I know it to be a
fable, which no man ever did or can prove.'
He explains that all that he had meant from
the beginning by 'separating from the Church,'
was refusing to 'go to church' ; and he proceeds as follows :—

'But here another question occurs : "What is the
Church of England ? " It is not all the people of
England. Papists and Dissenters are no part thereof.
It is not all the people of England, except Papists and
Dissenters. Then we should have a glorious Church
indeed! No : according to our twentieth Article, a
particular church is a " congregation of faithful people "

* Jackson's *Life of Charles Wesley*, vol. ii. pp. 394—396.

(*cœtus credentium* are the words of our Latin edition), "among whom the Word of God is preached, and the sacraments duly administered." Here is a true logical definition, containing both the essence and the properties of a church. What, then, according to this definition is the Church of England? Does it mean all the believers in England (except the Papists and Dissenters) who have the Word of God and the sacraments administered among them? I fear this does not come up to your idea of the Church of England. Well, what more do you include in the phrase? "Why, all the believers that adhere to the doctrine and discipline established by the Convocation under Queen Elizabeth." Nay, that discipline is well-nigh vanished away, and the doctrine both you and I adhere to.

'All those reasons against a separation from the Church in this sense, I subscribe to still: what, then, are you frighted at? I no more separate from it now than I did in the year 1758. I submit still (though sometimes with a doubting conscience) to "mitred infidels." I do indeed vary from them in some points of doctrine, and in some points of discipline (by preaching abroad, for instance, by praying extempore, and by forming societies); but not a hair's breadth further than I believe to be meet, right, and my bounden duty. I walk still by the same rule I have done for between forty and fifty years. I do nothing rashly. It is not likely I should. The heyday of my blood is over. If you will go on hand in hand with me, do. But do not hinder me, if you will not help me. However, with or without help, I creep on: and as I have been hitherto, so I trust I shall always be,

'Your affectionate Friend and Brother.' *

* Jackson's *Life of Charles Wesley*, p. 395: Smith's *History of Methodism*, vol. i., pp. 520, 521.

It is true that one of Wesley's latest sermons, that on ' The Ministerial Office,' preached in 1789, flames with indignation against unauthorised intruders into the office of the ' priesthood,' whom he compares to Korah and his fellows. But it must be remembered that he regarded ordination by himself, conferred on one of his preachers, as equally valid with any that might have been bestowed by the hands of any bishop of whatever Church. What he objected to in some of his preachers was that they had presumed to administer the sacraments *when he had not appointed them.* ' Did we ever appoint you,' he asks in his sermon, ' to administer sacraments, to exercise the priestly office ?' ' Where did I appoint you to do this ? Nowhere at all ! '

In the year preceding the date of the letter from which I have just quoted, Wesley had taken the necessary steps for organising an independent Methodist Church for America. His *Letter to Dr. Coke, Mr. Asbury, and our Brethren in North America*, is dated September 10th, 1784. In it he expounds his views as to Church government in strict agreement with the extract which I have quoted from the Disciplinary Minutes of 1747, making specific reference to Lord Chancellor

King's account of the Primitive Church; and he closes this letter with the following sentence :
' As our American brethren are now totally disentangled both from the State and from the English hierarchy, we dare not entangle them again, either with the one or the other. They are now at full liberty, simply to follow the Scriptures and the Primitive Church ; and we judge it best that they should stand fast in that liberty wherewith God has so strangely made them free.' For which reason, among others, Wesley had no desire, in 1784, that ' the English bishops should ordain part of our preachers for America.' *

Nevertheless in 1775, writing to a Tory statesman, Wesley described himself as ' a High Churchman, the son of a High Churchman ' ; and this fact is sometimes brought forward as evidence that he retained through life, substantially unchanged, the principles of his Oxford ritualistic Churchmanship. The more, however, the question is investigated, the more untenable will any such view appear. Wesley was never a political Low Churchman. He had no Dissenting predilections or Puritan punctilios or latitudinarian laxity. He was a Tory in Church and State. But during the last forty or fifty years of his life he altogether

---

* *Works,* vol. xiii., pp. 238, 239.

abandoned the positive principles of High
Churchmanship, both in theology and in relation to ecclesiastical government. The letter
to which I have referred was, however, one in
which he was justified in putting prominently
forward his Toryism, as regarded from a
political point of view, in order that he might
the better commend the argument of his letter
to the attention of a Tory statesman. He
was writing to Lord North on behalf of the
revolted American colonists, urging counsels
to which it would have been well if the
Government had listened. He was writing on
a political question to a politician. Accordingly he says, 'Here all my prejudices are
against the Americans; for I am a High
Churchman, the son of a High Churchman,
bred up from my childhood in the highest
notions of passive obedience and non-resist-
ance.' These words indicate the scope and
bearing of the High Churchmanship of which
he speaks. And yet it is curious how he goes
on to illustrate, even in the political sphere,
the independence and the liberal tone of his
Toryism. He proceeds thus : 'And yet in
spite of all my long-rooted prejudices, I cannot avoid thinking, if I think at all, these, an
oppressed people, asked for nothing more than
their legal rights, and that in the most modest

and inoffensive manner that the nature of the thing would allow.' *

His actual position in regard to High Church and Low Church, to Anglicanism and Nonconformity, is very clearly indicated in the following passages. In his journal, under date Friday, March 13th, 1747, he writes, ' In some of the following days I snatched a few hours to read *The History of the Puritans.* I stand in amaze; first, at the execrable spirit of persecution which drove those venerable men out of the Church, and with which Queen Elizabeth's clergy were as deeply tinctured as ever Queen Mary's were; secondly, at the weakness of those holy confessors, many of whom spent so much of their time and strength in disputing about surplices and hoods, or kneeling at the Lord's Supper.' † In April, 1754, again, he writes, ' I read Dr. Calamy's *Abridgement of Mr. Baxter's Life.* In spite of all the prejudices of education, I could not but see that the poor Nonconformists had been used without either justice or mercy, and that many of the Protestant bishops of King

* Smith's *History of Methodism,* i., p. 700.
† Compare also what he says in his letters to ' Mr. John Smith ' (Archbishop Secker), about ' Mr. Cartwright, and the body of Puritans in that age.' *Works,* xii., p. 82.

Charles (the Second) had neither more re- .
ligion nor humanity than the Popish bishops
of Queen Mary.' * But still more decisive,
perhaps, as to the limited and modified sense
in which alone Wesley could be regarded as
a High Churchman, even when he described
himself as such, is the following passage,
written two years later than his letter to Lord
North, viz., in 1777. In it he is, notwithstanding his letter of 1775, appealing to Dissenters to show loyalty to the King in the
struggle then going on with the revolted
colonies ; and he exclaims, ' Do you imagine
there are no High Churchmen left ? Did they
all die with Dr. Sacheverell ? Alas ! how little
do you know of mankind ! Were the present
restraint taken off, you would see them swarm-
ing on every side, and gnashing upon you
with their teeth. . . . If other Bonners and
Gardiners did not arise, other Lauds and
Sheldons would, who would either rule over
you with a rod of iron, or drive you out of the
land.' †

These passages seem to settle the question
as to Wesley's High Churchmanship. A Low
Churchman he was not, nor would he have
been in sympathy with modern Low Churchmanship, if he were living to-day. He dis-

* *Works*, ii., p. 297.   † *Works*, xi., pp. 132, 133.

liked Calvinism; he loved the cathedral service. But far less would he have been in sympathy with the Romanising Churchmanship of the present time. How far Wesley was, in taste and sympathy, from that kind of Low Church-manship which might have been described as Dissent in the wrong place, and which aimed at making the Church service and worship resemble as much as possible, in style and spirit, the service of the Calvinistic meeting-house, will be seen from the following outburst in a letter addressed, in 1778, to one of his most esteemed correspondents, Miss Bishop :

'But to speak freely, I myself find more life in the Church Prayers than in any formal extemporary prayers of Dissenters. Nay, I find more profit in sermons on either good tempers or good works than in what are vulgarly called Gospel sermons. The term has now become a mere cant word. I wish none of our society would use it. It has no determinate meaning. Let but a pert, self-sufficient animal, that has neither sense nor grace, bawl out something about Christ or His blood, or justification by faith, and his hearers cry out, "What a fine Gospel ser-mon!" Surely the Methodists have not so learned Christ.' *

* *Works*, xiii., p. 34.

But, on the other hand, it is evident that
Wesley was in utter antagonism with all that
is essential in modern High Churchmanship.
On points of principle, as distinguished from
taste and feeling, he was a Low Churchman—
he was an Arminian Low Churchman.

There is one short, sharp test which settles
this question. The High Churchman of to-
day rests upon his 'apostolical orders,' his
'succession'; this at any rate holds true of all
sacramentarian and ritualistic High Churchmen. Whereas the Low Churchman relies
upon the articles, the homilies, and the
general spirit of the common worship of the
Church. He is an illogical and inconsistent
Low Churchman who mixes up with these
things the properly High Church dogma of
the 'uninterrupted succession.' Now, on
which side was Wesley? We have seen that
he makes short work with 'the succession,'
as 'a fable which no man ever did or can
prove.' But yet more clearly and definitely
Low Church is the following remarkable passage, written in 1755 : 'My conclusion, which
I cannot yet give up, that it is lawful to continue in the Church, stands, I know not how,
without any premisses that are to bear its
weight. I know the original doctrines of the
Church are sound ; I know her worship is in

the main pure and scriptural. But if "the essence of the Church of England, considered as such, consists in her orders and laws" (many of which I myself can say nothing for) "and not in her worship and doctrines," those who separate from her have a far stronger plea than ever I was sensible of.' * Could Low Church principles cut lower than this?

In his journal, under date June 11th, 1739, little more than twelve months after his conversion, Wesley, in a letter which he there prints, thus sets forth the principle which guided him, a principle from which he never afterwards departed:

'You ask, "How is it that I assemble Christians who are none of my charge, to sing psalms, and pray, and hear the Scriptures expounded? and you think it hard to justify doing this in other men's parishes, upon catholic principles." Permit me to speak plainly. If, by catholic principles, you mean any other than scriptural, they weigh nothing with me; I allow no other rule, whether of faith or practice, than the holy Scriptures: but, on scriptural principles, I do not think it hard to justify whatever I do. God in Scripture commands me, according to my power, to instruct the ignorant, reform the wicked, confirm the virtuous. Man forbids me to do this in another's parish; that is, in effect, to do it at all; seeing I have now no parish of my own, nor probably ever shall. Whom then shall I hear, God or man? If it be just to obey man rather than God,

* *Works*, xiii., p. 185.

judge you. A dispensation of the Gospel is committed
to me ; and woe is me if I preach not the Gospel. But
where shall I preach it upon the principles you mention ?
Why, not in Europe, Asia, Africa, or America; not in
any of the Christian parts, at least, of the habitable
earth. For all these are, after a sort, divided into
parishes. If it be said, " Go back then to the heathens,
from whence you came : " nay, but neither could I now
(on your principles) preach to them ; for all the
heathens in Georgia belong to the parish either of
Savannah or Frederica. Suffer me now to tell you my
principles in this matter. I look upon all the world
as my parish; thus far I mean, that, in whatever part
of it I am, I judge it meet, right, and my bounden
duty to declare unto all that are willing to hear, the
glad tidings of salvation.'

Perhaps, on the whole, Wesley in his intermediate and indeed isolated position as a
Churchman, resembled the late Archdeacon
Hare in his relation to parties in his generation, as much as any other man that might be
named. But it is impossible to find a good
analogy for a position which in reality was
quite unique. A striking illustration of the
reality and thoroughness of the change which
passed upon John and Charles Wesley after 1738
is afforded by the manner in which from that
date to the end of his life—a period of thirty-
five years—their intimate and cherished friend
Clayton absolutely denied and ignored them
both. Mr. Tyerman says in his *Oxford Metho-*

dists (p. 55) 'John Wesley, between the years 1738 and 1773, visited Manchester more than twenty times; and some of these visits were so memorable, that Clayton must have heard of them; and, yet, there is not the slightest evidence of any renewal of that fraternal intercourse which was interrupted when Wesley began to preach salvation by faith only, and, in consequence, was excluded from the pulpits of the Established Church. This was heresy too great for a High Churchman to overlook. To be saved by faith in Christ, instead of by sacraments, fasts, penances, ritualism, and good works was an unpardonable novelty, deserving of Clayton's life-long censure; and hence, after 1738, the two old Oxford friends seem to have been separated till they met in heaven.' Mr. Tyerman shows that Wesley's first visit to Manchester after his conversion was in May, 1747, but though he preached at Salford Cross, immediately adjoining Clayton's residence, there is nothing to show that the former friends met for a moment. On Good Friday, 1752, Wesley went to the Old Church in Manchester, where 'Mr. Clayton read prayers; I think the most distinctly, solemnly, and gracefully of any man I ever heard.' The sacrament was administered, but though there is every reason

G

to suppose that Wesley was a communicant
and Clayton one of those who administered,
we do not find any recognition between them.
Three years later, in October, 1756, Charles
Wesley writes in his journal: 'My *former*
friend Mr. Clayton read prayers at the Old
Church, with great solemnity.' The same
week he adds, 'I stood close to Mr. Clayton
in church (as all the week past), but not a
look would he cast towards me; "so stiff was
his parochial pride," and so faithfully did he
keep his covenant with his eyes, not to look
upon his old friend when called a Methodist.'
Next day he heard Mr. Clayton preach a good
sermon on Constant Prayer. The senior
chaplain invited Charles Wesley to join the
other clergy in receiving the bread and wine
before the people, yet even after this public
recognition was vouchsafed by his senior
Clayton seems to have taken no notice of his
old friend.

CHAPTER IV

RELATIONS OF WESLEY, AS A METHODIST, AND OF
PRIMITIVE METHODISM, WITH THE CHURCH OF
ENGLAND.

WE have seen how far Wesley had travelled
since 1738. The investigation which
we have thus far conducted is fundamental to
any correct view of the relations of Methodism
to the Church of England. There are some
who still hope that a violent and entire breach
between Methodism and the Church of England may yet be averted. But of this there
can be no hope, if the position and the principles of Wesley himself are for ever to be
misunderstood. Those who at the same time
summon Methodists, on the authority of their
founder, to return to the fold of the Church
of England, and deny to their pastors and
preachers the status of ministers, both mistake
the facts of the case, so far as Wesley himself
was concerned, and do all that lies in their
power, so far as modern Methodism is concerned, to widen separation into alienation,
to harden and provoke independence into
animosity and antagonism. Wesley had plans

G 2

—dreams many may think them—by which he conceived that the Methodist organisation, as such, might in great part have been attached to the Church of England, might have been the means of largely reviving that Church, of absorbing not a little of explicit and professed Dissent, of making the Church living and national throughout the land. He feared that, if this did not come to pass, if nothing were done by the rulers of the Church towards meeting his views, his people would, after his death, become a separate people. In his independent organisation of American Methodism, he had embodied in general his own ideal of an independent Methodist Church. He knew full well the mind of many of his leading preachers, headed by Dr. Coke, as to the high benefit and desirableness, if not the necessity, of Methodism in England becoming an independent organisation. But he desired to postpone such a consummation as long as possible, and to prevent it if possible; he was bent upon securing for his own Church the utmost space and opportunity for effecting an organic union with his societies. He endeavoured so to use his influence to the last as to keep as many of his people attached to the Church as possible, and at least to preclude a separation on Dissenting principles.

It is wonderful how long and how far his influence has extended. Even such a policy as that represented in the pastorals of the late Bishop of Lincoln (Dr. Wordsworth), and exemplified in the outrage some years ago inflicted by the vicar of Owston Ferry, has not fully availed to drive Methodism to make a breach with the Church of England. It may yet be possible, by a wise and generous policy, to retain many friends in the Methodist Connexion who hold that it is well, apart from all voluntary communions, to have a liberal Protestant Established Church, or who, at all events, are opposed to a disestablishment agitation. But it is no more possible, by quoting the authority of Wesley, on the one hand to win back, than it is by petty persecutions on the other to drive back, any appreciable number of Methodists into the ranks of the Church. All that such conduct can do is to irritate and alienate at large.

In fact the principles which Wesley embraced in 1738 determined all his future course, and every step he afterwards took looked towards separation and independence, unless, in good time, Methodism could somehow be taken up into organic union with the Church of England and yet left as a system in its substantial integrity. It is evident, from the terms of the Deed of Declaration, by which, in 1784, he legally constituted the Conference, that Wesley contemplated the possibility of the chief ministers in some of his circuits being stationary ordained clergymen of the Church of England, with and under whom itinerant Methodist Evangelists might do the work of the 'circuits.' The limitation of a preacher's labours in connection with the same chapel to a period of three years as provided by that Deed does not apply, according to the terms of the Deed itself, in the case of an ordained clergyman. Wesley's dream, probably, was that a number—an increasing number as years passed on—of Methodist preachers might be appointed to benefices situated respectively at the head place or in the centre of the 'circuits' of Methodism, and that, living there, they might act as the chief ministers of such circuits, having unordained itinerants as their subordinate colleagues and coadjutors. The celebrated Mr. Grimshaw, vicar of Haworth, and the still more celebrated Fletcher of Madeley, did thus act as the chief ministers of Methodist circuits, and had their names as such upon the *Minutes of Conference.* If this process had gone on, these ordained Methodist clergy being members of the Conference, there might conceivably have been a Methodist order and organisation within the Church of England, of which the members, distinguished by zeal and activity, might have been extending their lines and labours in all directions. I can see no necessary reason why something like this might not have taken place ; the orders of the Church of Rome have done a work somewhat analogous, have had their own assemblies, their special organisation and discipline, their generals. Wesley had early studied closely, and has left on record his admiration of, the genius and discipline of Loyola. And it was, perhaps, his highest desire to do, in a frank and evangelical sense and spirit, for the Church of England, a work somewhat resembling what Loyola had organised with such marvellous success for the Church of Rome. Whatever might, however, have been his ideas in regard to this matter, they were not to be fulfilled ; and, apart from such fulfilment, the steps he successively took were directly bent, as I have said, towards one goal—the goal of separation, of organised independency.

When (in 1739) Wesley organised a system of religious societies, altogether independent of the parochial clergy and of episcopal control, but dependent absolutely on himself, he took a step towards raising up a separate communion, especially as the ' Rules ' of his societies contained no requirement of allegiance to the Established Church. When (in 1740) he built meeting-houses, which were settled on trustees for his own use, and when (in 1741) he began (with his brother) to administer the sacraments in these houses, a farther step was taken in the same direction. His calling out lay preachers (in 1741) wholly devoted to the work of preaching and visitation, was still a step in advance towards the same issue.* The yearly Conference (begun in 1744) tended obviously in the same direction. The legal constitution of the Conference in 1784, and the provision for vesting in trustees for the use of the ' People called Methodists,' under its jurisdiction as to the appointment of ministers and preachers, all the preaching places and trust property of the Connexion, was a most important measure, giving to the Union of the societies a legally corporate character and large property rights. The

---

* When this step was challenged, he met the challenge in a style which shows how radical an anti-High Churchman was Wesley. ' I do assure you, this at present is my chief embarrassment. That I have not gone too far yet, I know; but whether I have gone far enough, I am extremely doubtful. . . . Soul-damning clergymen lay me under more difficulties than soul-saving laymen.'—*Works*, xiii., p. 197.

ordination of ministers, even for America,* as Charles Wesley pointed out forcibly at the time, could hardly fail to conduct towards the result which Wesley had so long striven to avert—viz., the general ordination of his preachers in Great Britain. If it was necessary to ordain for America, they would plead that it was highly expedient to ordain for England. The principle was conceded, the only question was one of time and fitness as to its more extended application. The ordinations for Scotland† were refused by Wesley so long as he could refuse them with either safety or consistency. Without them his people would, in very many cases, have been left quite without the sacraments, as the Calvinistic controversy had become embittered, and Wesley and his followers were accounted heretics by the orthodox in Scotland. Nevertheless, ordaining for Scotland could not but hasten the day when preachers must be ordained for England. It was hard to require that Mr. Taylor should administer in Scotland and hold himself forbidden and unable to administer in England. And when at length Wesley was compelled to ordain a few ministers for England,‡ it could

---

* In 1784.   † In 1785.

‡ In 1788 he ordained Alexander Mather deacon, elder, and superintendent or bishop ($\epsilon\pi\acute{\iota}\sigma\kappa\sigma\pi\sigma\varsigma$), and on

not but be seen that what had been done in the case of the few could not always be refused as respected their brethren at large. As little could it be expected that while for various reasons, in addition to London and Bristol, which had enjoyed this privilege from the beginning, more and more places were allowed to have preaching in church hours, the concession of the same privilege to other places that might desire it could be permanently denied.

In weighing this summary of facts, Churchmen are also bound in justice to remember that it was the continued refusal of the clergy in Bristol to administer the Lord's Supper to the Methodists, and even to the Wesleys themselves, which drove the brothers to administer it to the 'societies' in their own meetinghouse. Similar conduct constrained Wesley to allow separate services in more and more places, and, in the end, to ordain some of his own preachers to assist him in administering the sacraments to his societies even in England.

Ash Wednesday, 1789, he ordained Henry Moore and Thomas Rankin presbyters, and empowered them to administer the sacraments to the Methodists of England. (See an able article on 'The First Principles of Early Methodism' in the *London Quarterly Review* for January, 1884).

It was in 1755 that the demands of the preachers and the societies for the administration of the Lord's Supper among themselves, and by the hands of the preachers, first began to make themselves powerfully felt. Wesley had much ado to resist the importunities of his flock, which were enforced with much feeling and with the weight of strong reasons. Such men as Thomas Walsh and Joseph Cownley—that is to say, the very best of his preachers—headed this movement. For five, ten, fifteen years they had been preaching, and the societies had grown up to maturity under their pastoral care and instructions. It was no wonder if they felt that the pastoral character of those who were *de facto* the ministers of the churches ought to be completed ; and it is very much to the credit of these excellent men and able preachers that considerations of Christian expediency, forcibly urged by John Wesley, prevailed with them to hold their claims in abeyance, and to labour on—in some cases for more than thirty years afterwards—as mere preaching deacons. Those who wish to understand fully all that belongs to this interesting section of Methodist history must study the pages of Mr. Jackson, in his *Life of Charles Wesley.* It was in connection with this that the controversy began between

Wesley and his brother Charles, some of the last passages in which, thirty years later, have been already referred to. Mr. Jackson says :

'The year 1755 was a sort of crisis in Methodism, because then a controversy on these subjects began, which was not finally settled until some years after the founders of the system had ended their life and labours. In London and Bristol the Lord's Supper was regularly administered by a clergyman; but in most other places both the preachers and the societies were expected to attend this ordinance in their several parish churches. In many instances the clergy who officiated there were not only destitute of piety, but were immoral in their lives; and doubts arose, whether such men, notwithstanding their ordination, were true ministers of Christ, and whether it was not a sin to encourage them in the performance of duties for which they were so manifestly destitute of the requisite qualifications. The clergyman at Epworth, who repelled Mr. John Wesley from the Lord's Table, and assaulted him before the whole congregation, was notoriously drunk at the time. In other cases, the doctrine which was taught in the churches was deemed not only defective but positively erroneous; especially when justification by faith, and the work of the Holy Spirit, were peremptorily denied and opposed. Several of the clergy were directly concerned in the instigation of riotous proceedings against the Methodists, by which their property was destroyed, and their lives were endangered; and if the sufferers forgave these injuries, it was too much to expect that they would contentedly receive the memorials of the Saviour's death at the hands of men who had encouraged such outrages upon humanity and justice. If John Nelson could profitably receive the Holy Communion from the minister who, by bearing false witness against him, had succeeded in tearing him away from his family, and sending him into the army, every one had not John's meekness and strength of mind. Not a few of the clergy absolutely refused to administer the Lord's Supper to the Methodists. When these people approached the table of the Lord, they were singled out among the communicants and denied the sacred emblems of their Redeemer's body and blood. This was the case, as we have seen, at Bristol, at Leeds, in Derbyshire, and other places; so that the Methodists were compelled either to receive the Lord's Supper at the hands of their own preachers, or in the Dissenting Chapel, or to violate the command of the Lord, who has charged all His disciples to " eat of this bread and drink of this cup." Great uneasiness therefore existed among the preachers, and in several of the societies.' *

In regard to what was determined upon at the Conference of 1755, Wesley wrote to his brother as follows :—

'Do not you understand that they all promised by Thomas Walsh, not to administer, even among themselves ? I think that a huge point given up ; perhaps more than they could give up with a clear conscience.

'They showed an excellent spirit in this very thing. Likewise when I (not to say you) spoke once and again, spoke *satis pro imperio*, when I reflected on their answers, I admired their spirit, and was ashamed of my own.

'The practical conclusion was, not to separate from the Church. Did we not all agree in this ? Surely either you or I must have been asleep, or we could not differ so widely in a matter of fact.

* Jackson's *Life of Charles Wesley*, vol. ii., pp. 68, 69.

'Here is Charles Perronet raving, because "his friends have given up all"; and Charles Wesley, because "they have given up nothing"; and I, in the midst, staring and wondering both at one and the other.

'I do not want to do anything more, unless I could bring them over to my opinion : and I am not in haste for that.

* * * * * *

'Thomas Walsh (I will declare it on the house-top) has given me all the satisfaction I desire, and all that an honest man could give. I love, admire, and honour him; and wish we had six preachers in all England of his spirit. But enough of this. Let us draw the saw no longer, but use all our talents to promote the mind that was in Christ.

'We have not one preacher who either proposed, or desires, or designs (that I know) to separate from the Church at all. Their principles in this single point of ordination I do not approve; but I pray for more and more of their spirit (in general) and practice.

'Driving me may make me fluctuate; though I do not yet.'*

Much is made by many Churchmen of the injunctions which Wesley so often gave to his people down to his last days, not to separate from the Church of England. There can be no doubt that he had a passionate desire to keep them as long as possible, and as many of them as possible, within that fold; but no injunctions or entreaties on his part could change the logic of facts or prevent the neces-

* *Wesley's Works*, xii., pp. 108, 110.

sary consequences of the course he himself pursued so steadily for fifty years. Besides, his sayings on the other side were sharp and strong, and cannot but have the more weight as having been wrung from him in spite of himself, in spite of the strongest bias in the other direction. Writing to his brother Charles, Wesley says, in 1755, in a letter from which I have already quoted : ' Joseph Cownley says, " For such and such reasons I dare not hear a drunkard preach or read prayers." I answer, *I dare*, but I cannot answer his reasons.' And again, writing still to his brother thirty years later, in 1786, he says : ' The last time I was at Scarborough I earnestly exhorted our people to go to church, and I went myself. But the wretched minister preached such a sermon that I could not in conscience advise them to hear him any more.'*

It is truly said, and much stress is laid upon this point, that Wesley urged his preachers and people not to hold their services in church hours. This was his rule; but it is equally true that in London and Bristol, his chief centres, the services had almost from the beginning been held in church hours, that he sanctioned many other exceptions to the rule,

* *Works*, xii., pp. 109, 144.

and that the number of exceptions increased as the years went on, until at length, in 1788, general liberty was given to hold such services wherever the people did not object, except only on Sacrament Sunday. This exception was absolutely necessary, because, as a rule, Methodists could only obtain the sacrament at church. As yet but few of the preachers were ordained. Wesley and Coke, Wesley's lieutenant after his brother Charles ceased to itinerate, could rarely visit any given place, and they never visited some places. Local preachers supplied the pulpit, leaders met the classes; but neither could administer the sacraments.

Wesley's views as to the Established Church were—as has been shown—very lax. Regarded as a National Church, he defined it to be merely a political institution. He seems to have considered that every one who believed the main doctrines of the Church of England and lived a Christian life, according to his best lights and opportunities, so long as he did not consciously or deliberately dissent from that Church, was to be regarded as a member of it.* We must bear this in mind if we would understand how it was that Wesley, at

* Wesley's letter to his brother Charles in 1785, quoted on p. 70.

the same time, earnestly desired and entreated his people generally to remain as closely as possible attached to the Church of England, and yet, whenever any usage, or customary right, or even law, of that Church seemed to come into conflict with what he regarded as the spread of evangelical truth and life, was prepared to make an entire and unhesitating sacrifice of it. He regarded the Church of England, indeed, and all belonging to it as only a means to an end. Hence, in 1755, when his brother Charles was trembling and indignant in the prospect, as he foreboded, of a speedy and organic separation of many of the preachers and of the societies from the Church, Wesley wrote to him thus :—

'Wherever I have been in England the societies are far more firmly and rationally attached to the Church than ever they were before. I have no fear about this matter. I only fear the preachers' or the people's leaving, not the Church, but the love of God, and inward or outward holiness. To this I press them forward continually. I dare not, in conscience, spend my time and strength on externals. If, as my Lady (Huntingdon) says, all outward Establishments are Babel, so is this Establishment. Let it stand for me. I neither set it up nor pull it down. But let you and I build up the city of God.'*

* *Works,* xii., p. 110.

H

Again, still more notable are his words already quoted at the end of the last chapter :—

‘ My conclusion, which I cannot yet give up—that it is lawful to continue in the Church—stands, I know not how, without any premisses that are to bear its weight. I know the original doctrines of the Church are sound ; I know her worship is, in the main, pure and Scriptural. But if the “essence of the Church of England, considered as such, consists in her orders and laws ” (many of which I myself can say nothing for) “ and not in her worship and doctrines,” those who separate from her have a far stronger plea than I was ever sensible of.’

Again, in 1786, writing to his brother, Wesley said, ‘ As you observe, one may leave *a* church (which I would advise in some cases) without leaving *the* Church. Here we may remain in spite of all wicked or Calvinistic ministers.’ In the same year, a month earlier, he had written, also to his brother, ‘ Indeed, I love the Church as sincerely as ever I did ; and I tell our societies everywhere, “ The Methodists will not leave the Church, at least while I live.” ’†

The limitation intimated in the last clause quoted is not without significance. But there were occasions on which Wesley contemplated the possibility of actual Dissent, even on his own part, although assuredly no alternative,

* *Works*, xiii., pp. 185, 186. The date is 1755.
† *Works*, xii., pp. 144, 145.

no extremity could well have been more repugnant to all his tastes and feelings. The Bishop of London having excommunicated a clergyman for preaching without a license, Wesley wrote respecting this, ' It is probable the point will now be determined concerning the Church, for if we must either dissent or be silent, *actum est.*' ' Church or no Church,' again he wrote, ' we must attend to the work of saving souls.'*

It was at last brought to the sharp issue which Wesley dreaded—so far as many, and in the end all, of his congregations were concerned. They were obliged either to *dissent or be silent.* One of Wesley's latest letters, addressed to a bishop, relates to this subject. The Methodists found themselves forced either to register their meeting-houses as ' Protestant Dissenting ' places of worship, or else to forego all the protection and benefits of the Toleration Act. I give the Methodist patriarch's letter entire. He was eighty-seven years old when he wrote it.

' MY LORD,—It may seem strange that one who is not acquainted with your lordship should trouble you with a letter. But I am constrained to do it ; I believe it is my duty both to God and your lordship. And I

* Stevens' *History of Methodism*, i., p. 398.

must speak plain, having nothing to hope or fear in this world, which I am on the point of leaving.

'The Methodists, in general, my lord, are members of the Church of England. They hold all her doctrines, attend her service, and partake of her sacraments. They do not willingly do harm to any one, but do what good they can to all. To encourage each other herein, they frequently spend an hour together in prayer and exhortation. Permit me, then, to ask, *cui bono?* "For what reasonable end" would your lordship drive these people out of the Church? Are they not as quiet, as inoffensive, nay, as pious as any of their neighbours, except perhaps here and there a harebrained man who knows not what he is about? Do you ask, Who drives them out of the Church? Your lordship does, and that in the most cruel manner, yea, and the most disingenuous manner. They desire a license to worship God after their own conscience. Your lordship refuses it, and then punishes them for not having a license! So your lordship leaves them only this alternative, "Leave the Church or starve." And it is a Christian, yea, a Protestant Bishop that so persecutes his own flock. I say persecutes, for it is a persecution to all intents and purposes. You do not burn them, indeed, but you starve them. And how small is the difference! And your lordship does this under colour of a vile, execrable law, not a whit better than that *De Hæretico Comburendo.* So persecution, which is banished out of France, is again countenanced in England.

'O my lord, for God's sake, for Christ's sake, for pity's sake, suffer the poor people to enjoy their religious as well as civil liberty. I am on the brink of eternity. Perhaps so is your lordship too. How soon may you also be called to give an account of your stewardship to the great Shepherd and Bishop of our souls! May He enable both you and me to do it with joy! So prays, my lord,

'Your lordship's dutiful son and servant.'*

Thus were the Methodists compelled, against their own will, as well as sorely against the will of their founder, to become, in legal construction, Protestant Dissenters.

Nevertheless, it is remarkable how slowly the process of actual separation proceeded. The date of the letter just quoted was June 26th, 1790, a few weeks before the last Conference at which Wesley presided. What effect the new condition of things might have produced on his views or conduct if he had been a younger man and had lived a few years longer, it is impossible to conjecture. He was still hoping for relief from this stringent and impolitic application of the Conventicle Act up to the date of his death. But it is certain that the Dissenting party within the Conference and among the societies (by no means a small or feeble party) must have been stimulated and strengthened by finding themselves forced into the legal position of Dissenters. Nevertheless, the spirit of Wesley prevailed in the councils of his followers after his death to a degree which, all things considered, is really surprising.

* *Works*, xiii., p. 137.

In 1787 Wesley had said, ' When the Methodists leave the Church of England, God will leave them ' ; in 1788, that the ' glory ' of the Methodists had been ' not to be a separate body,' that they ' would not be a distinct body,' and that ' the more he reflected the more he was convinced that the Methodists ought not to leave the Church'; in 1789, that ' none who regarded his judgment or advice would separate from the Church of England.' And as a matter of fact, notwithstanding the enforcement of the Conventicle Act, the Conference after Wesley's death did not ' separate from the Church of England.'

What Wesley dreaded first and most in separation was its want of charity, its schismatic temper and tendency. Many passages might be quoted to prove this. His whole soul revolted from the thought of his people deliberately, for reasons assigned, and upon a manifesto of dissent and separation, severing themselves from the Church. If there were to be separation, his determination all through life was, that the separation should be imposed and forced upon, not sought or determined by, the Methodists. He could not but be aware, moreover, that the conscious and deliberate organisation of his people into a separate Church would be in many ways a hazardous and precarious experiment. He was persuaded that the express adoption by himself and his people of the status and principles of a Dissenting sect would bring disorganisation and ruin to Methodism.

Wesley knew indeed that what he had done amounted to partial separation from the Church of England, regarded as an organised body, and that this separation was very likely to spread farther and farther; he knew that he had done a number of things, each of which contained the principle of a complete separation, unless the Church of England should take some special means of reform and comprehension, to prevent such a separation, and to gather into organic connexion the churches of Methodism. His longing was that such means might be taken : and as long as it was possible, he would, for his part, keep the door of hope for union open. His object was not division or separation, but revival and re-animation. Hence his invincible opposition to all proposals for express and general separation from the Church. If separation was to ensue, he would leave the blame of it entirely on the supineness or the intolerance of the Anglican clergy. His hand, at least, should not sever the tie. He knew, however, that after his death, unless

a change came over the character and policy
of the clergy, a separation must ensue before
long. He knew that the very steps he had
taken had shown the way to effect such a
separation : and he never repented of those
steps, although he saw most clearly whither
they pointed. Had the Church known the
day of her visitation, no separation need have
ensued. If it did not, a separation was in-
evitable, and even desirable ; and it was
necessary that the way wisely to provide
against such a contingency should be indicated. Besides, every one of the steps he had
taken had been imperatively forced upon him
by the necessities of his evangelical labours.
Providence had indicated them. The work
must have been brought to a stand without
them. And if, through the obstinacy of the
Church of England, the steps thus forced
upon Wesley were to prepare the way for
a separation, this also must be right, and in
the order of Providence.*

* The following extract from Wesley's Journal,
under date August 4th, 1788 (*Works*, vol. iv.), will illustrate what is said in the text :—' The sum of a long
conversation [at the annual Conference] was—1. That
in the course of fifty years we had neither premeditatedly
nor willingly varied from it in one article of doctrine
or discipline. 2. That we were not yet conscious of
varying from it in any point of doctrine. 3. That we

John Wesley had striven to hope, like his brother, that through the wisdom of the bishops some way might be devised for preserving Methodism in its spirit and discipline, and yet keeping the Methodists in communion with the Church of England, and making Methodism subsidiary to that Church—a source to it of life and power. But years passed on, and all his intimations were rejected; it became more and more evident that Methodism was producing little or no change within the recognised precincts of the Church itself; and that the clergy and their bishops, with very few exceptions, were determined to frown upon Methodism; while the needs of the people of

have in a course of years, out of necessity, not choice, slowly and warily varied in some points of discipline, by preaching in the fields, by extemporary prayer, by employing lay-preachers, by forming and regulating societies, and by holding yearly Conferences. But we did none of these things till we were convinced we could no longer omit them, but at the peril of our souls.' It must be admitted, however, that the list of 'variations' is very formidable, and that it would be difficult to discover in what respect, for fifty years, Wesley had adhered, as a clergyman, to the discipline of his Church. He had been constrained, in fact, to found a separate community, established on principles and informed with a spirit altogether in contrariety to the principles and spirit of the Anglican Establishment.

England still pressed as before, and the demands of his own societies at home and abroad to have provided for them the due administration of the holy sacraments were continually becoming more general and more resolute. Under these circumstances Wesley was obliged, however reluctantly, to ordain some of his preachers. We have seen what the case of America was; that of Scotland was scarcely less clear, the Methodists there could not well be members of Calvinistic churches; in parts of England, where crowds of Methodists found only profane, often insulting, clergymen, it was impossible—it would have been monstrous—continually to withstand their demand. Wesley did withstand the demands of many of his people, and the convictions of not a few of his best preachers, so long as to drive a considerable number both of the preachers and people outright into Dissent. Mr. Edwards founded an Independent church at Leeds, Titus Knight one at Halifax, John Bennet a number in Lancashire, Charles Skelton one at Southwark, and so forth. It is quite certain that, but for the sacramental ministrations of the Wesleys, of the few clergymen who assisted them, as Grimshaw, Fletcher, and Dickinson, and of the few preachers whom he ordained, the number of Independent churches formed out of Methodist churches would have been much greater. And after Wesley's death, if the preachers had not at length, after some years of turmoil and intense excitement, yielded to the reasonable demands of the people, and consented to allow the sacraments to be administered in those societies in which otherwise peace could not have been preserved, it is certain that tens of thousands of Dissenters would have been added to the ranks of those who were opposed on principle to the Established Church.

The Conference, as I have said, after Wesley's death acted in harmony with the spirit of their founder. Even the enforcement of the Conventicle Act, the hardships of which were not removed till 1812, when Lord Liverpool passed an Act repealing the obnoxious and oppressive restrictions on the liberty of preaching, did not drive them into any extreme course. They suffered indeed, between 1791 and 1795, the peace of the Connexion to be most seriously embroiled, and allowed many of their churches to be brought to the verge of dissolution, before they consented to permit even the gradual extension of separate services in church hours and of sacramental administration by their own preachers for the members of the ' societies.'

In giving this guarded permission they still did but follow the precedent of Wesley, and act in conformity with his spirit and principles. They never at any time decreed a separation of Methodism from the Church of England ; that separation was effected by the particular societies distributively and the individual members personally, not at all by the action or on the suggestion, but only by the permission, of the Conference. The Wesleyan Conference did not in fact recognise and provide for the actual condition of ecclesiastical independency into which the Connexion had been brought until that condition had long existed; and Methodist preachers abstained from using the style and title appropriate to ordained ministers, and from assuming in any way collectively the language of complete pastoral responsibility, until by the universal action of the Connexion the 'societies' had, of their own will, practically separated themselves from the Church of England and forced their preachers into the full position and relations of pastors —pastors in common of a common flock, who recognised them alone as their ministers and amongst whom they itinerated by mutual arrangement.

Looking at the whole evidence, it appears to be undeniable that, so far as respects the

separate development of Methodism, Wesley
not only pointed but paved the way to all that
has since been done, and that the utmost
divergence of Methodism from the Church of
England at this day is but the prolongation
of a line the beginning of which was traced
by Wesley's own hand. It is idle to attempt
to purge Wesley of the sin of schism in order
to cast the guilt upon his followers. There is,
indeed, neither sin nor, properly understood,
schism in the case, unless it be that the sin of
persecution and proscription may be charge-
able on some of the ministers and people of
the Church of England. But at any rate
Wesley himself led his people into the course
which they have since consistently pursued.

It is, at the same time, no less undeniable
that separation was the necessary result of
Wesley's work, because the Church of England
failed to make any provision—in fact it made
no effort towards providing—for the incor-
poration of Methodism within its own system.

CHAPTER V.

AFTER Wesley's death, the preachers trod most strictly in the steps of their founder; they breathed the self-same spirit: they 'walked by the same rule'; they 'minded the same thing.' They took no step towards independence which was not forced upon them; they passed no resolution or law declaring or compelling separation. As many of the Methodists as chose were not only at liberty, but by the majority of the preachers were encouraged, to attend their parish church, and to take the Sacrament from the parish priest. And for many years after Wesley's death a large proportion of the Methodists continued so to do. Only by degrees, and through individual conviction and preference, were the Methodists as a community actually separated from the Church of England.*

After Wesley's death, indeed, the feeling which the venerable founder of Methodism

* See Joseph Benson's letter to Mr. Thompson of Hull in 1800.

had, for many years, experienced the greatest difficulty in repressing, and which many among his preachers, and vastly more among his people, had only suppressed out of deference to the feelings and authority of one whom they regarded as their bishop and patriarch, broke out with overwhelming force. The people demanded what they could not but regard as their evangelical right—that the sacraments should be administered to them by those who had so long been their pastors and preachers. A number of trustees—men of property, in many instances; in others, Methodists that had been, who had become Church formalists ; in some cases, good, single-eyed, conservative followers of ' Old Methodism ' —and most of the preachers, were at first opposed to the people's demands. Year by year, however, the feeling of the societies became stronger and more unanimous ; the opposition of the trustees sank away ; the preachers became convinced that the people's demands must either be conceded, or Methodism altogether broken up, leaving no permanent result except a multitude of scattered Dissenting congregations. The Conference and the itinerancy would have been destroyed. Dissent would have been enormously strengthened ; the name of the Established Church

would have been rendered intolerable to mul-
titudes. Accordingly, after a resistance pro-
tracted for four years, it was settled at the
Conference of 1795, that, where a majority of
the stewards and leaders in any society, and
also of the trustees of the chapel, desired it,
the Lord's Supper might be administered.
No society was advised to ask for this; the
tone of the Conference to the last was rather
dissuasory; but provision was made that,
society by society, where the members insisted
on the sacraments being administered, they
should be administered. This is all the separation from the Church of England which has
ever taken place in Methodism. It took five-
and-twenty years to consummate the result.
That result was that the ministers finally came
to administer the Sacrament in every circuit
and every society.

This result was hastened by the intolerance
of many of the clergy and also by the religious
indifference, and, too often, the open miscon-
duct, of many more. In 1800, according to
the concurrent testimony of Churchmen themselves, the clergy at large were little, if at all,
superior to what they had been fifty years before.

It is now the policy of Churchmen to
allege that Wesley was a Churchman to the
last, and that, if Wesleyans were consistent,

they would be Churchmen too. Fifty years
ago, Churchmen took very different ground,
and argued that Wesley was, throughout all his
active career, a ' schismatic,' and no other than
a Dissenter, whatever he might fancy himself
to be. The facts are quite as much in favour
of this view as of that now set forth by our
modern Churchmen.

Truth, however, on the whole gains through
these discussions. Feeling and opinion oscil-
late from one extreme to another ; but there
is progress notwithstanding towards an equit-
able and comprehensive settlement of the
question. Churchmen now admit that the
corruption and supineness of their Church in
the middle of the last century were such as to
justify irregularities ; they admit, moreover,
and lament that Wesley and his people were
coarsely and often cruelly driven out from a
communion in which he and his brother, most
honestly and intensely, and many of his people
very seriously, desired to remain. Further
still, they justify by the schemes and proposals
which, even at the present day, they set forth
for the comprehension of Methodism, notwithstanding its separate existence for more than
half a century, those ideas and hopes as to the
possibility of retaining Methodism within the
Church, if the bishops and clergy had but

I

been willing, which the Wesleys ventured to indulge.

All this is so far good ; it is eminently satisfactory to Methodists ; it is accompanied with many indications of Christian candour and kindliness on the part of Churchmen which ought to be frankly and cordially acknowledged and reciprocated. It remains only for them to learn two things—that Wesley ceased to be a High Churchman five-and-forty years before his death, and that Wesleyan Methodism cannot be absorbed. The former point is, as I venture to affirm, settled by this investigation ; the second may be said to be a direct consequence from the first, but is, besides, rendered certain by other considerations.

Methodism, as I have noted in an early part of this volume, if it were to be 'reconciled' to the Church of England, would have to part company with the other Christian churches and communions throughout the world. The liberty of friendship and co-operation which it now enjoys would have to be given up. From a large and wealthy place, where almost all evangelical churches can meet, it would have to retire into a very strait room.

The genius of Methodism, as now fully organised into a church, and that of Anglican

Episcopacy are mutually repellent and exclusive. In the Church of England everything depends absolutely upon the bishop or the minister, or, as they say, 'the priest.' This is not the case in Methodism. No leader can be appointed without the concurring vote of the Leaders' Meeting, nor any local preacher be admitted on trial or into full recognition except on the resolution and by the vote of the Local Preachers' Meeting. The power of discipline is, to a large extent, in the hands of the Leaders' Meeting. No member can be censured or expelled, unless he has been found guilty at a Leaders' Meeting, or by a committee of the Quarterly Meeting. No minister can be introduced into the pulpit of a Methodist chapel who has not been recommended to the ministry by the Quarterly Meeting of the circuit to which he belongs. All this, I apprehend, is contrary to the essential principles of the Church of England. How could these provisions be fitted into harmony with an organisation in which the sole and absolute power of the clergy, as such, to admit to communion or to repel, is, however it may be in practical abeyance, a fundamental principle, and in which the law of patronage remains supreme? Moreover, it would be impossible for the Church of England to admit all

Methodist ministers, merely as such, to take full pastoral rank and authority in the administration of the sacraments. To do so would be to renounce the dogma of sacerdotal succession, and to admit that the validity of orders has no relation to episcopal authority. And, on the other hand, it is certain that neither the Methodist people nor their ministers would endure a word of re-ordination, or consent to the relinquishment of the right of sacramental administration.

Besides, it is just as likely that Methodism should absorb Anglican Episcopacy as that Anglican Episcopacy should absorb Methodism. Methodism has already, within the network of its own sister or daughter churches, a more widespread and a more numerous ' connexion ' and communion of churches—a vaster host of adherents—than Anglican Episcopacy can sum up in all its branches and correlatives. As a world-power, Methodism is the more potent in its operation and influence. For the Church of England (so called) now to absorb Methodism would be a portentous operation. It would be more hazardous than to put new wine into old bottles.*

* In a letter which appeared in the *Times* in September, 1867, the Rev. L. H. Wiseman furnished the following statistics :—' In the United Kingdom there

But surely, in a l reason and modesty, the Church of England should heal her own breaches before her Congresses give sittings to consider how to effect the inclusion and reconciliation of Nonconformists within her own pale. There are three parties within the Church of England—High, Broad, and Low.

are belonging to the original Wesleyan society 356,727 recognised and registered members. Careful inquiries have shown that for every member three other persons may be added, either as regular hearers though not avowed members, or as children of members who are being brought up in the faith of their parents; thus giving a total of a million and a half of adherents. In Australia, the West Indies, Canada, and other colonies where the English language is spoken, the number calculated in the same way will be about 573,000 more The several bodies which have separated on disciplinary grounds—none of them on any doctrinal ground—from the original society, number in England and the colonies 288,000 members, or 1,152,000 adherents. It will thus be seen that in England and its dependencies considerably over three million persons are attached to the Methodist communions. If we turn to the United States a recent return places the membership of the Methodist Episcopal Church at 1,700,000; the numbers cannot be given at present with absolute exactness from some of the churches in the South. It is generally estimated, however, in the United States that this Church numbers not less than seven million adherents; and there are, in addition, as is the case in England, minor bodies which have separated from the parent Church, though still holding the Methodist

If the High are to reconcile Nonconformists
with themselves, Nonconformists must embrace Apostolic Succession and sacramental
efficacy—in fact, embrace that which, in its
essentials, is Popery. If the Nonconformists
are to be reconciled on the principles of the
Low-Church, they must contrive to harmonise
evangelical Calvinism or Arminianism, as the

name and discipline, whose followers may be estimated
at a million more. Putting all these members together,
it will appear that the several branches of the Methodist communion number between eleven and twelve
million persons in those countries where the English
language is spoken. Taking the same area of com-
parison, what now is the number of adherents of the
Anglican communion ? To begin with the United
Kingdom, it is well known that in Scotland and Ireland they form only a small part of the population;
but in England they probably equal all the Noncon-
forming bodies put together. . . . Allowing for Ireland
and Scotland, it appears a fair calculation to allow to
her eight millions of adherents in the United Kingdom.
As to the colonies, computation is difficult. Throughout Canada and Australia the number of Methodist
clergy and places of worship greatly exceeds the number belonging to the Church of England ; for example,
the number of Methodist clergy in Canada last year
was 1,003, and of Anglicans, 479 ; but let it be supposed that the number of Churchmen in the colonies is
a million, or nearly double the number we have put
down for the Methodists, and let the Anglicans in the
United States, whose communicants have been estimated at 250,000, be put down at a million or a million

case may be, with the Prayer-book, if not also with the fabulous hypothesis of Apostolical Succession, which, fascinating dream as it is to most Churchmen, is held by some even among the Low-Church clergy. If, again, Nonconformists are to be reconciled on the principles of the Broad-Church, they must make up their minds to accept a latitude of faith and construction in matters of religion which tends to dissolve all definite theology and all distinctions between faith and unbelief, between the Church and the world, which does away with all Church discipline and with all real and earnest Christian fellowship.

In good sooth, however, there are but two theories on which the Church of England can, as a matter of principle and of right, affect to

and a half more, the total number of adherents will then be ten millions or ten millions and a half against the eleven millions and upwards belonging to the Methodists.'

The following tables confirm Mr. Wiseman's calculations, and enable us to supply corrections to the present time: The statistics for 1870 are taken from a German History of Methodism, published by Dr. Jacoby, a German minister of the American Methodist Episcopal Church, which is described as 'an interesting and comprehensive work,' and is published at the Book Room of the Methodist Episcopal Church at Bremen; those for 1884 are from the American Methodist Almanac for 1886 :—

GENERAL VIEW OF METHODISM IN DIFFERENT PARTS OF THE WORLD.

The figures marked * with an asterisk are approximate, as no official report is to hand.

EUROPE.	Members 1870.	Members 1884.	Ministers 1870.	Ministers 1884.	Local Preachers 1870.	Local Preachers 1884.	Sunday-school Scholars 1870.	Sunday-school Scholars 1884.
GREAT BRITAIN.								
Wesleyan Methodists	367,306	445,638	1,565	1,917	10,470	14,183	601,801	879,112
Wesleyan Methodists in Ireland	20,699†	25,457	175 }	237	{ 1,600	2,000*	17,653 }	32,000*
Primitive Wesleyans in Ireland	9,000 }		125 }		{ 300 }		10,000* }	
Primitive Methodists	161,229	191,108	913	1,044	14,169	15,982	258,857	400,000*
Methodist New Connexion	26,309	33,819	163	215	1,119	1,271	68,592	78,500*
United Methodist Free Church	68,062	83,469	312	415	3,445	3,330	152,315	200,000*
Bible Christians	26,241	30,034	254	241	1,759	1,909	44,221	60,000*
Wesleyan Reformers	8,650	8,771	23	15	600	600*	18,056	18,200*
FRANCE,								
French Wesleyan Methodists	2,158	1,797	52	31	117	127	2,768	2,219
English Wesleyan Methodists	1119	271	3	13	37	2	168	576
SPAIN AND PORTUGAL.								
Wesleyan Methodists	37	406	2	9	—	11	275	455
ITALY.								
Wesleyan Methodists	790	1,512	4	28	61	22	743	691
GERMANY.								
Methodist Episcopal Church	6,956	9,000*	56	80*	29	52*	7,434	16,500*
Wesleyan Methodists (Evangelical Association included in America)	1,015	2,226	11	27	53	138	261	2,686
DENMARK, SWEDEN, & NORWAY.								
Methodist Episcopalians	1,100	1,300*	19	25*	30	37*	564	700*
AMERICA.								
BRITISH POSSESSIONS.								
Wesleyan Conference in Canada	66,877 }	168,803	580 }	1,628	250* }	1,959	53,024 }	125,000*
East British American Wesleyan Conference	16,291 }		160 }		119 }		15,742 }	
Methodist Episcopalians	28,957	2,100	216	45	224	—	24,000*	21,000*

UNITED STATES.								
Methodist Episcopal Church	1,291,404	1,787,339	7,330	12,811	10,278	12,211	1,163,839	1,796,031
Methodist Episcopal Church, South	535,681	877,299	2,495	4,045	4,431	5,869	500,000*	400,000*
African Bethel M. E. Church	200,000	391,014	550	1,882	1,50†*	9,740	150,000*	130,000*
African Zion M. E. Church	64,800	300,009	694	2,000	700*	2,750	75,000*	110,000*
Coloured Methodist Episcopal	100,000*	125,000	—	638	—	681	—	—
Protestant Methodists	25,000	130,000	800*	1,500	800*	1,010	90,000*	111,000*
Wesleyan Methodists	—	23,590	236	207	164	215	23,000*	15,000*
Evangelical Association (including Canada and Germany)	60,211	119,758	478	953	982	509	40,855	118,000*
United Brethren in Christ	108,122	159,547	861	1,257	783	963	106,002	135,000*
Sundry Small Methodist Societies	55,000*	44,975	200*	353	200*	578	45,000*	61,000*
WEST INDIES.								
Wesleyan Methodists	43,902	50,669	90	107	370	510	21,577	29,434
ARGENTINE REPUBLIC.								
Methodist Episcopal Church	151	151*	7	7*	—	—	290	300*
ASIA.								
CHINA.								
Methodist Episcopal Church	1,415	1,800*	17	23*	64	72*	265	350*
Wesleyan Methodists	104	783	11	19	4	3	312	574†
INDIA.								
Methodist Episcopal Church	578	—	41	—	33	—	3,711	—
Wesleyan Methodists	635	2,924	33	64	13	98	5,333	17,545‡
CEYLON.								
Wesleyan Methodists	1,980	4,341	30	66	58	153	3,765	11,556
AFRICA.								
LIBERIA.								
Methodist Episcopal Church	1,830	2,300*	15	23*	38	45*	1,240	1,700*
BRITISH COLONIES, *including Missions to Heathens.*								
Wesleyan Methodists	22,223	49,488	91	226	733	1,964	17,195	28,062
AUSTRALASIA. **BRITISH COLONIES,** *including Missions to Heathen.*								
Wesleyan Methodists	61,175	74,391	228	482	2,786	4,430	118,222	146,049
Methodist New Connexion (other Methodist Societies included in Great Britain)	8,329	1,448	97	35	155	—	6,824	10,000*
TOTAL	3,360,166	5,154,701	19,019	32,729	57,934	83,616	3,654,215	4,979,196

† These Churches are united.   ‡ Day and Sunday Scholars.

reclaim to itself all 'the Sects.' These are
—the High-Church theory, which demands
submission from all as of right, and counts
Nonconformity to be the deadly sin of schism ;
and the Broad-Church theory, according to
which the Church is co-extensive with the
nation, and every Englishman, as such, is a
member of Christ.

Methodists equally repudiate both theories.
They reject the superstitious mediævalism
of the one, and they detect the intrinsic un-
Christianity, however disguised, of the other.
They understand by schism an uncharitable
division in a church, not a necessary separation from it; and they pray themselves, on
behalf of the Church of England, tainted as
it is with Romanising superstition, and dis-
tracted with incurable divisions, that God
would be pleased to deliver it from 'false
doctrine, heresy, and schism.' They do not
desire to see Christendom distributed into
merely National Churches, which could not be
truly spiritual communities, nor to see one only
church prevail, whatever might be its name,
although they would not needlessly multiply
denominations. They would leave the free
influence of the truth, under the power of the
Spirit, so to mould and adapt Churches in the
midst of nations and of the world, as to exhibit

the Gospel and its fellowship according to the several aspects and modes best adapted, on the whole, to bring out into living power the manifold variety and fulness of the Gospel, and to produce the highest and richest total effect upon the nations and the world at large. Cherishing no hostility or animosity against the Church of England—desiring for it nothing worse than that it should be freed from all essential germs of Popish superstition and spiritual despotism, and should undergo, without violence or spoliation, a salutary and effective reorganisation—Wesleyan Methodists decline, without thanks, though with respect and goodwill, all overtures whatsoever for reunion, or (which is the same thing) for absorption. They must 'abide in their lot' till 'the end of the days.'

APPENDIX.

The following is a list of books and pamphlets relating to the subjects with which I have dealt in the foregoing pages :—

Authorised Report of the Church Congress held at Wolverhampton, October 1—4, 1867. London : Macmillan and Co. 1867.

The Guardian Newspaper, Supplement, Wednesday, February 12th, 1868. Report of the Meeting of Convocation for the Province of York.

Methodism and the Established Church. By the Rev. WILLIAM ARTHUR, M.A. *London Quarterly Review for July*, 1856.

The First Principles of Early Methodism and The Methodist "Plan of Pacification," 1791—1795. By the Rev. JOHN S. SIMON. *London Quarterly Review, January and October*, 1884.

Life of Rev. Charles Wesley, M.A. By THOMAS JACKSON. Two vols. 8vo. London : Wesleyan Conference Office. 1841.

An Answer to the Question, Why are you a Wesleyan Methodist? By THOMAS JACKSON. Sixth Edition. London : Wesleyan Conference Office. 1860.

The Church and the Methodists. Being the Substance of a Speech addressed to the Wesleyan Conference in 1834. By THOMAS JACKSON. Wesleyan Conference Office. 1834.

The Life of Peter Böhler. By the Rev. J. P. LOCKWOOD. *With an Introduction on the Early Religious Life of the Wesleys.* By the Rev. THOMAS JACKSON. Wesleyan Conference Office, 1868.

The Question, Are the Methodists Dissenters? Fairly Examined. By SAMUEL BRADBURN. 1792.

A Reply to a Pamphlet, entitled, 'Considerations on a Separation of the Methodists from the Established Church.' By HENRY MOORE. Bristol. 1794.

The Crisis of Methodism; or, Thoughts on Church Methodists and Dissenting Methodists, including Strictures on Mr. KN*X's 'Considerations,' and 'Candid Animadversions, &c.' By JONATHAN CROWTHER, P.G. Bristol. 1795.°

Primitive Methodists, an Address from the Trustees of Broadmead and Guinea Street Chapels in Bristol to the Methodist Conference, and to all the Societies, &c. Published by Order of the Trustees. Bristol. (Dated July, 1795.)

A Vindication of the People called Methodists, in Answer to a 'Report from the Clergy of a District in the Diocese of Lincoln,' in a letter to Thomas Thompson, Esq., of Hull. By JOSEPH BENSON, a Preacher among the Methodists. London. 1800.

The Church and the Wesleyans. Their Differences shown to be Essential. Oxford: J. H. Parker. 1843.

Pastoral Advice of the Rev. John Wesley, M.A. London: Masters and Co.

The Church and Wesleyanism. A Letter by the Rev. P. G. MEDD. London: Rivingtons. 1868.

The Church and the Methodists. By the Rev. C. HOLLAND HOOLE. 1868.

* P.G. stands for 'Preacher of the Gospel.' Mr. Bradburn's pamphlet, of which the title is given above, is a most acute and masterly compendium of the whole question. Nothing can be more skilful than the way in which, without a word wasted or the colour of exaggeration, he puts his points; and nothing can be finer than the spirit in which he writes. His argument is exhaustive. He shows, amongst other things, that if the authorities of the Church of England had been willing, it might have been possible to accomplish, during Wesley's life-time, such a union of Methodism with the Established Church as is now desired by such Churchmen as Mr. Medd and Mr. Lyttelton.

Occasional Papers of the Home Reunion Society. Nos. 1—5. 7, Whitehall. 1878.

History of Wesleyan Methodism. Three vols. By G. SMITH, LL.D. London : Longmans.

History of Methodism. By ABEL STEVENS, D.D. Three vols. New York. London: Trübner and Co.

John Wesley, the Church of England, and Wesleyan Methodism. Their relation to each other clearly and fully explained in two dialogues. I. *Was John Wesley a High Churchman?* II. *Is Modern Methodism Wesleyan Methodism?* London: The Wesleyan Methodist Book-Room. 1883.

www.ingramcontent.com/pod-product-compliance
Lightning Source LLC
Chambersburg PA
CBHW031157050726
47495CB00019B/2353